"Hold it right there. I've got a gun and I'm not afraid to use it."

Kody raised his arms in the air, then turned to locate the source of danger. He almost chuckled at the sight before him. A thin, brown-haired woman, eyes steady, mouth set in a hard line. She held a rifle almost as long as she was tall.

"You ain't gonna shoot me."

"Back off or you'll see what I mean to do," she said.

Kody took one swift step forward and plucked the rifle from her. He cracked it open to eject the bullet. The chamber was empty. "Lady, you sure got guts."

"This is my house. Get out."

She lived here? In a deserted house? Alone?

"*Your* house, huh?"

"My brother's. I'm watching it for him."

"Don't look like it needs much watching." The room was about as bare as the miles of windswept fields he'd ridden by. It didn't take a lot of looking to see the place was vacant. Except for this woman. "What's anyone going to take?"

Books by Linda Ford

Love Inspired Historical

The Road to Love
The Journey Home

LINDA FORD

shares her life with her rancher husband, a grown son, a live-in client she provides care for and a yappy parrot. She and her husband raised a family of fourteen children, ten adopted, providing her with plenty of opportunity to experience God's love and faithfulness. They had their share of adventures as well. Taking twelve kids in a motorhome on a three-thousand-mile road trip would be high on the list. They live in Alberta, Canada, close enough to the Rockies to admire them every day. She enjoys writing stories that reveal God's wondrous love through the lives of her characters.

Linda enjoys hearing from readers. Contact her at linda@lindaford.org or check out her Web site at www.lindaford.org, where you can also catch her blog, which often carries glimpses of both her writing activities and family life.

LINDA FORD

The Journey Home

Steeple
Hill®

Published by Steeple Hill Books™

STEEPLE HILL BOOKS

Steeple
Hill®

ISBN-13: 978-0-373-82794-7
ISBN-10:   0-373-82794-6

THE JOURNEY HOME

www.SteepleHill.com

Printed in U.S.A.

Preserve me, O God, for in thee do I put my trust.
—*Psalms* 16:1

This book would not be what it is without the help of several key people:

First, my editor, Melissa, who saw what it needed. Thank you for your guidance and encouragement.

And then two very dear critique partners who listen to me whine and still find ways to point out what I'm doing right and where I should reconsider my direction. To Debbie and Carolyne, thank you both for your continued support, your friendship and your helpful suggestions. If I dedicate every book to you it's because I couldn't do it without you.

Chapter One

South Dakota, 1934

He didn't know why God answered his prayers any more than he could explain why he still said them. But there it stood, the protection he'd moments ago begged God to provide, an old farmhouse, once proud, now with bare windows and a door hanging by one hinge. Deserted by the owners, as were so many places in the drought-stricken plains. The crash of '29 had left hundreds floundering financially. And years of too little rain resulted in numerous farms abandoned to the elements. He didn't hold out much hope of 1934 being any different.

Kody Douglas glanced upward. The black cloud towering high into the sky thundered toward him. An eerie yellow light filled the air. A noisy herald of birds flew ahead of the storm. Kody ducked his head against the stinging wind and nudged Sam into a trot. They'd better get inside before the dust storm engulfed them.

In front of the house, he leaped from the saddle, led Sam across the worn threshold and dropped the reins to the floor. Sam would remain where he was parked until Kody said otherwise, but still he felt compelled to make it clear. "You stay here, horse. And don't go leaving me any road apples. You can wait to do that business outside."

He grabbed the rattling door and pushed it shut. A hook hung from the frame. The eye remained in the door, and he latched it.

"Probably won't hold once the wind hits," he told his ever patient mount and companion. Man got so he talked to the only living, breathing thing he shared his day with.

Kody snorted. You'd think a man would get used to being alone. Seems he never could. Not that he cared a whole lot for the kind of company he encountered on the trail. Scoundrels and drifters willing to lift anything not tied down. Kody might be considered a drifter, but he'd never stoop to being a scoundrel. He had his standards.

He yanked off his hat and slapped it against his thigh, creating his own private cloud of dust.

He jammed the hat back on his head and glanced around. Place couldn't have stood empty for long. No banks of dirt in the corners or bird droppings on the floor. The windows were even still intact.

The wind roared around the house. Sam tossed his head as the door banged in its crooked, uncertain state. Already the invading brown dust sifted across the linoleum. The air grew thick with it. The loose door wouldn't offer more than halfhearted protection, and Kody scanned the rest of the house, searching for something better.

"Don't go anywhere without me," he told Sam as he strode through the passageway into a second room. The drifting soil crunched under his boots.

Again, God provided more than he asked and certainly more than he deserved. A solid door stood closed on the interior wall to his right. He could shelter there until the duster passed. He yanked open the door.

"Hold it right there, mister. I've got a gun and I'm not afraid to use it," a voice cracked.

Kody's heart leaped to his throat and clutched at his tonsils. His nerves danced along his skin with sharp heels. Instinctively he raised his arms in the air, then slowly, cautiously, turned to locate the source of danger. He almost chuckled at the sight before him. A thin, brown-haired woman pressed into the corner, eyes steady, mouth set in a hard line. She held a rifle almost as long as she was tall.

The upward flight of his arms slowed and began a gradual descent. "You ain't gonna shoot me." It was about more'n she could do to keep the rifle level. The business end wobbled like one of those suffering trees in the wind outside.

"Back off or you'll see soon enough what I mean to do."

He lowered his right arm a few more inches, at the same time taking one swift step forward.

She gasped as he plucked the rifle from her.

He cracked it open to eject the bullet. The chamber was empty. He roared with laughter. "Lady, you got more guts than a cat stealing from a mother bear." Amusement made his words feel round and pleasant in his mouth. Unfamiliar, even. It'd been a long time since he'd done more than growl his words. He pulled his gaze from the woman who triggered the amusement, knowing his keen look made her uncomfortable.

She jutted out her chin. "This is my house. Get out."

She lived here? In this deserted house? Alone?

He stilled the questions pouring to his thoughts to deal with the immediate concern. "I don't intend to go out in a blinding dust storm. And no God-fearing, decent woman would expect me to."

She swallowed his accusation noisily. But nothing in her posture relented from her fierce protectiveness.

"I mean you no harm." Without seeking her permission, he sauntered to the corner farthest away, leaving her to plot her own actions. He made like he didn't care what she did, though his every nerve danced with alertness. Might be she had a hunk of wood hid beneath her skirts and would sneak up on him and smack him hard enough to give him a headache to regret. He didn't much figure she could overpower him even with a weighty length of two-by-four. He held back a heartfelt chuckle. Gotta admire a woman with so much spunk.

He heard her slight hiss and from the corner of his eyes saw her take a faltering step toward the door, maybe more intent on escape than anything.

The wind shook the house. The light faded. Through the window he watched the black cloud envelop them. Dust billowed through the cracks around the frame. They needed something to cover the window. In the dim light he made out a pile of material on the floor and, ignoring the woman's indrawn breath, went over to investigate. A ragged quilt. "Why don't you have this over the window? It might keep out some of the dirt."

"What a wonderful idea. I should have thought of it myself." Her sarcasm nearly melted the paint off the wall.

He snorted. "That is a most uncharitable attitude."

She put a rag to her nose. "How do you suggest I get it to stay there? Or do you propose to hold it in place?"

"Ma'am, where there's a will there's a way." What a sharp-tongued young woman. He held the quilt to the window. It greatly reduced the amount of dust coming through the cracks. A nail at one corner served as a hook. He felt around but could find no nail on the other corner. He pulled at the frame. It fit too tightly to allow him to stuff the material behind it. He stood with his arms over his head feeling as exposed as a deer in the middle of a bare field. And he was about to put himself into an even more vulnerable position. "You happen to have a fork or knife handy I could jab in behind the frame and hold this in place?"

She crossed the room and handed him a nail. "It fell out and I couldn't get it back in."

The quilt darkened the room, but even in the dim light he immediately saw her problem. She barely came up to his armpit. She'd need something to stand on to reach the top of the window. She probably needed a stool to brush her teeth. He grinned at his silly imagination and plucked the nail from her fingers. But how to drive it in? "Hold this."

He scooted over to make room for her. She lifted her arms and pressed the quilt as high as her short stature allowed. He felt around the window until he found a crack between the frame and the wall and wedged the nail in as firmly as he could. He caught a corner of the quilt over it and stepped back. "That should do."

"Thank you," she muttered as she headed back to the corner.

He chuckled. She sounded about as grateful as if he'd handed her a bucket of sand. He returned to the opposite side of the room and hunkered down.

"Your house, hey?"

"My brother's. I'm watching it for him."

"Don't look like it needs much watching." The room was about as bare as the mile after mile of windswept fields he'd ridden by. It didn't take a lot of looking to see the place was vacant. Except for this woman. "What's anyone going to take?"

She made a sound that could have been anger or a signal of her intent to argue, but the storm increased in ferociousness. She ducked her head instead.

He pressed his hankie to his nose and prepared to wait it out.

* * *

Charlotte huddled into the corner. He'd accused her of being uncharitable. Her own thoughts rebuked her for being sharp-tongued. Normally she was neither, but her patience had worn thin, and her fears fueled by unexpected, unfair circumstances. Her faith had been sorely tested of late. Tested but not abandoned. What else did she have left but her trust in God?

Our Father, who art in heaven… She closed her eyes and silently repeated the words, mentally squeezing each for strength, determined to think of nothing but God's love and power.

But a dust storm raged outside, sifting fine particles of dirt through the air, threatening to drydrown her, and inside sat a strange man. Her nerves twitched with anxiety greater than she'd known even on her first night alone in the empty house.

And not just any man. An Indian, complete with braids and a feather dangling from his cowboy hat.

I will not fear. God is with me. He will never forsake me.

The words had become her daily supplication since she'd walked into the house and found it empty—her brother, Harry, her sister-in-law, Nellie, and the two children had disappeared.

She'd been at the Hendersons' with instructions from Nellie to help with the new baby. Upon her return she discovered them gone—lock, stock and kitchen supplies—and a note from Harry saying he couldn't take the drought any longer. They were going farther west. No room in the truck for her. He'd send for her soon, within a week for sure. He'd arrange for Mr. Henderson to deliver a message.

They'd left barely enough food and water to last her.

"God will take care of me," she murmured.

The frightening man turned. "You say something?"

"God will take care of me." She spoke louder, firmer. After all, He'd led the children of Israel through the desert. Her situation wasn't any worse. Except she was alone. No, not alone. God was with her. So she had reminded herself over and over.

The house shook under the wind's attack. Dirt ground between her teeth. Her throat tickled. She breathed slowly to stop the urge to cough. She longed for a drink. Her last drink had been some unsatisfying mouthfuls this morning. The only place she could get more was at Lother's. She shuddered just thinking of her nearest neighbor.

Eligible young men were scarce as rain. Most

had gone looking for work. Seemed wherever they went jobs were hard to come by. She saw them riding the rails every time she was in town, going from one end of the country to the other. Lother, one of the few bachelors still in the community, made it clear he'd be glad to marry Charlotte. He seemed to think she'd be equally pleased to accept the opportunity. If she had to choose between marriage to Lother or rotting on the manure pile, she'd gladly choose the latter. She shuddered again, harder.

"It will doubtless end soon."

Did he think she worried about the storm? That happened to be the least of her current concerns. "You can be certain? I heard tell they had a three-day duster over toward Bentley."

"Yeah, but it ended, didn't it? Even the flood ended eventually."

Despite her mental turmoil, she laughed. "I guess we should be grateful we haven't had a forty-day duster."

The wind increased in velocity.

The man raised his voice. "I sat by a railway track once while a train went by. Never figured wind could make more noise, but it does."

The roar made conversation impossible.

She hunkered down, prepared to wait out the storm. Just like she'd been waiting for Harry's message. Was she destined to spend her life waiting for one thing or another?

Kody glanced toward the woman. She sat with a rag of some sort pressed to her face. Above the gray cloth her eyes regarded him with wariness. Or was it determination? He guessed both. She'd already shown she had plenty of grit.

The wind grew louder. The room darkened like the dead of night. He buried his face against his knees and waited. Could be the storm would end soon, or not. No predicting the nature of nature. He smiled into his handkerchief. Ma would chuckle at his choice of words. Suddenly in the noisy gloom, he missed his mother and father, even though he knew they were better off with him out of the picture. Nor were they the only ones to benefit from his departure. He pushed aside the forbidden memory.

The woman opposite him coughed. Not a tickling sort of cough relieved with a clearing-your-throat kind of sound, but a dry cough that went on and on. He held his breath, waiting for it to end. She stopped and he let out a gust of relief. It was short-lived as she began again.

Poor woman needed some water to wash down the dust.

He slid across the floor until his elbow encountered the warm flesh of her arm, vibrating from her coughs. "Here, have a drink." He offered her the canteen he'd grabbed out of habit, having learned never to wait out a dust storm without water nearby to wash his throat.

She latched on to the canteen, lifted it to her mouth and drank greedily. For a fearful moment he thought she'd drain the contents. Not that it was a matter of life and death. He'd refill it from her well as soon as the storm ended. But nevertheless he swallowed hard. A duster could make a man mighty thirsty.

She capped the canteen and handed it back. "Thank you."

He stayed where he was and again buried his face in his handkerchief and let his thoughts drift back to Favor, South Dakota, where he'd been born and raised and where the only parents he'd ever known still lived. He didn't want to think about all he'd left behind. Better to think about this woman huddled in the corner.

He turned his head a fraction, still protecting his face but making it possible to talk. "What's your name, ma'am?"

"What's yours?"

He chuckled. Got to admire a woman who showed no fear even in this awkward and potentially threatening situation. He knew many men who would take advantage of his position—alone with an unprotected woman. "Ma'am, my name is Kody Douglas. My father is a preacher man and I've been raised to be honorable and God-fearing." The "raised" part was true. Never mind he no longer had the faith he'd been raised with. Not that he could explain what he now believed. God's love had become so mixed up in his soul with man's unloving behavior he didn't know how to separate the two.

She uttered a sound full of disbelief.

He wasn't surprised. All his life he'd encountered the same reaction. As if a man like him could have a father like his, a home like his, a faith like he'd once had. For most people it defied explanation.

He hunkered down over his knees, preparing to ignore the woman. No doubt she likewise wished to ignore him. Besides, there was no reason to strike up a conversation. He'd be gone as soon as the storm ended. They'd never see each other again in this life or the one to come. That idea gave him pause. "You a believer?" he asked, even though he'd just told himself conversation was unnecessary.

"In God?"

He grunted affirmation.

"Most certainly I am. I have been since I was a

child at my mother's knee. In fact, He has been my strength and help all my life. He will continue to take care of me."

Kody wondered at the way she said the words. As if she expected him to argue. "Got no cause to disagree." God did seem to favor the likes of her, but Kody figured God regretted making the likes of him.

"My name is Charlotte Porter."

He thought of shaking her hand but refrained. He didn't want to put her in the position of having to choose whether or not to accept his offer nor did he want to shift his position and allow any more dirt to invade. Dust covered every bit of exposed skin, filling his pores until he envied the fish of the sea. He might head west to the ocean and sit in the water until he shriveled up like an old man just for the pleasure of having clean skin if he hadn't already decided to ride north into Canada and keep riding until he got to uninhabited land.

He settled for acknowledging her introduction with the proper words, though she perhaps expected nothing more than a grunt. "Pleased to meet you."

"You from round here?"

He guessed she felt the need of conversation more than he did. At least he wanted to believe so. Again he told himself a man should get used to being alone and sharing his thoughts with a faithful horse. "Not so's you'd notice." There was nothing about his past he wanted to share with this woman or anyone else on the face of the earth, and nothing about his future that held significance for anyone but himself.

"Where are you headed?"

"Just following my nose."

"Mr. Douglas, are you being purposely evasive?"

He chuckled. "Maybe I am. You might say it's a habit of mine." Seemed no need to refuse the woman the information she sought. "I'm from Favor, South Dakota."

"I never heard of an Indian preacher man." Her voice was muffled.

"I ain't no preacher man." He jerked his eyes open, felt the sting of dust and closed them again.

"I mean your father."

He kept his handkerchief to his mouth, guessed she kept her eyes closed, too, so she couldn't see his smile. "My father is a white man."

She twitched. "But—"

"My mother is white, too. Kind of defies explanation, doesn't it?" He squinted at her, saw her regarding him through narrowed eyes.

"That's impossible."

He laughed, liking the way her eyes momentarily widened, then as quickly narrowed against the dust.

"Not if I'm adopted. Besides, my real mother is white. My father…" He paused. "One look at me is all it takes to know he was Indian."

"Adopted? Well, that explains it, doesn't it?"

Her voice said so much more than her words. As if it mattered about as much as fly sweat. As if he was already gone and forgotten. He settled back into his own thoughts, not sure he liked the way she silently dismissed him. Didn't she have any particular opinion about his heritage, the unnaturalness of being raised white while looking native? Everyone else seemed to.

He wrenched his thoughts to more practical matters.

Had the light increased? Surely the wind roared with less vehemence. "It's letting up."

"Thank God. If this is the last duster I ever see, I would be eternally grateful."

"You and thousands of others."

Neither of them moved—gray dust particles in the air would fill their eyes and nose and lungs. No, they had to wait a bit longer. Kody glanced around the room, taking in more details. The only thing in the room was a bundled-up mattress in the corner.

"Why did your brother leave you here alone?"

"Who says I'm alone?"

He laughed. "I mean apart from me and my horse."

"I didn't mean you."

Again he laughed. This woman amazed him. Did she truly think he'd look around, see a virtually abandoned home and think she had a passel of brothers or sons or a husband to protect her? "What kind of brother leaves his sister alone?"

She studied him with narrow-eyed concentration. Weak light poked around the quilt at the window, but it didn't take morning sun on her face for him to know she resented his questions. But he couldn't dismiss his concern. Why would her brother leave her here alone? It didn't seem natural. For sure it wasn't safe. He wasn't the only man wandering about the countryside. Hundreds of them rode the rails every day looking for work or avoiding the realities of the Depression. Work was scarce. Pay even scarcer. He'd been trying for months to earn enough money to buy himself an outfit to start new in the North. He'd managed to save a few dollars. A few more and he'd be on his way.

"He's coming for me." She kept her face buried in her hands, the rag muffling her words. "Real soon."

"Until then you're here alone."

"I am not alone. God is with me. He has promised to be with me always."

Her words sifted through his thoughts, trickled down his nerves and pooled in his heart like something warm and alive. "I used to believe that."

"It's still true whether or not you believe it."

He laughed softly into his hands at the solid assurance in her voice. Could she really be so convinced? He stole a look at her. She regarded him. He wished he could see her mouth. Would it be all pruned up sourlike, or flat with determination?

She lowered her hand to speak and his eyes widened in surprise at the faint smile curving her lips. "One thing I know about God is He is unchanging. He doesn't have moods or regret or uncertainty as we often do." She turned enough to see the window and seemed to look right through the quilt and see something special beyond the fabric and glass. "'Fear not: for I have redeemed thee, I have called thee by thy name; thou art mine. When thou passest through the waters, I will be with thee; and through the rivers, they shall not overflow thee: when thou walkest through the fire, thou shalt not be burned; neither shall the flame kindle thee.'"

His heart burned within him. Had he not heard the words from his parents' lips time and again? *I have called thee by name. Thou art mine.* Yet somehow they sounded more convincing coming from this woman. He almost believed them.

Chapter Two

The man scrambled to his feet. Charlotte stood, as well, feeling as if every pore held a spoonful of irritating sandy dirt. Oh, for a good bath. Oh, for a quenching drink of water. For three days she'd metered out the last drops of her supply. Apart from a few swallows this morning, she'd had only the warm drink from the man's canteen.

She swiped at her hair, scrubbed the dirty rag over her face, shook her skirts and coughed.

The man slapped his hat against his leg and filled the air with a swirl of dust. She coughed again.

"Sorry," he muttered. "I should have waited until I was outside."

Charlotte threw open the door and choked on the thick air. The floor lay buried in several inches of dirt. The outside door must have ripped from its hinges. She closed the solid wood, blocking her only escape route. "Person can't breathe out there yet."

She kept her face toward the knob, thought of ushering the man out to his destiny. But his remark about the charity of a Christian woman still echoed in her head. She'd give him a few more minutes, then she'd rush him on his way. Presuming he'd allow her to rush him. If he didn't… No point in threatening him with the rifle. Anger scalded her throat. If Harry had had the decency to leave her a bullet or two, she'd have had no trouble getting rid of the man in the first place.

Maybe she could appeal to his decency. After all, his parents were white folk and religious, so surely the man had been raised to know right from wrong. Of course the same could be said about a lot of men who nevertheless chose wrong. The thought erased every vestige of calmness.

She heard him move about the room and stiffened as he approached her bedroll. Harry and Nellie had left her bedding and enough food for a week. How very kind of them.

"Where are you headed from here, Mr. Douglas?" She hoped he'd hear the urgent suggestion in her words.

"Kody, if you please. I'm going wherever I can find work."

She ignored his suggestion she call him Kody. Father or son, made never mind to her. He'd soon be riding the tail of the wind out of her house and out of her life. Couldn't be too soon to suit her. "I expect you'll have to ride some to find work. It's mighty scarce around here. Lots of folks pulling up stakes and moving on."

"My sentiments exactly. It's an unfriendly country in my opinion."

At the harshness of his voice, she turned to study him. The typical angular high cheekbones, lips pulled into a hard, unyielding line that spoke of determination. "I take it you've been as disappointed in life as many of the folks around here." Harry and Nellie among them.

He faced her full on, his black eyes steady as if measuring her.

She met his gaze, knew they both had secrets bringing them to this place, this time and this house. She believed God cared for her, controlled every aspect of her life. Didn't the Scripture say all the days of her life were written before one of them came to be? But right now she struggled to believe it. How could God have planned for the country to blow from county to county? For Harry to abandon her? For a half-breed to be in her house? But she was being overly dramatic. Harry would send for her as he'd promised. He'd taken care of her since she was ten and their mother grew too ill to manage on her own. He'd provided her with a safe home since Mother died, as he'd sworn he would—apart from that time Nellie had demanded she be sent away. Charlotte shuddered. She would never forget her subsequent ordeal at the Appleby home.

Anxious to escape the past as much as the present, she opened the door again, breathing shallowly as she picked her way over the dirt on the floor.

Mr. Douglas followed close on her heels, whistling when he saw the damage in the front room. "Looks like your brother could plant a garden in here."

She ignored his comment. Her brother wouldn't be planting a garden anywhere near this house. And God willing, she'd shake off the dust of the place this very afternoon and be on her way to join him. Out of habit and desperation, she went to the window to see if Mr. Henderson rode her way with the promised letter from Harry. But she saw only the changed landscape—mounds of dirt in new places, fields scraped clean in others. A desolate, angry scene.

"Lady, could you point me to your well? I'd like to wash this storm off my face and refill my canteen."

She turned away from the hopeless view. His face looked as if he'd scrubbed in garden soil. She touched her cheeks, guessing she looked no better. "Well's out there." She pointed to the little shack Harry had built to store tools in.

Kody tromped into the kitchen.

Charlotte followed and screamed as she came face-to-face with a paint horse.

"This is Sam," Kody said. "He won't hurt you."

"You brought your horse into my house?" She sniffed. "Phew. He's stunk up the place like a barn."

Kody shook his head. "Sam, I told you not to do that in here."

The horse whinnied.

Charlotte thought the sound as unbelieving as her thoughts. "A horse answers the call of nature without regard to his surroundings."

"I'll clean it up."

"You certainly will." And she'd scoop out the dirt with the only tools Harry had left her—a tin can and a big spoon.

Kody grabbed the empty bucket from the old worktable left behind because it was nailed to the wall. He headed for the well. He had the decency to lead his horse outside with him and kick out the pile of manure as he left.

Charlotte stood at the door, praying for a

miracle. God had brought water from a rock for His children in the desert. Didn't seem like water from the well ought to be any different. And while He was providing miracles, maybe He could see fit to send a message from Harry and something to send Mr. Douglas hightailing it out of here.

Kody walked with a combination of roll and stride. He grabbed the handle and pumped up and down. The squealing protest caused Sam to sidle away and whinny. After several unproductive pumps, Kody called, "Well appears to be dry."

Charlotte sighed. Hoping against hope proved futile yet again. She couldn't imagine what lesson God meant for her to learn. "I know."

He sauntered over. "Been dry long?"

She shrugged. He didn't need to know the particulars, but they'd been going to Lother's for water for several months.

Kody shook the bone-dry pail. "Where was your brother getting water?"

Charlotte stared across the pasture indicating a well-worn path. In the distance she could make out the chimney, the roof of the barn and the life-saving windmill. "Lother Gross has been kind enough to let us use his well."

Kody touched his cheek with a brown finger. "I'd like to wash and refill my canteen." He waited, perhaps expecting her to lead the way.

Why couldn't the man take a hint? Desperately she sought for a way to persuade him to leave. The gun was out unless she used it as a club, and she didn't much fancy the idea of attacking him, knew she didn't stand a chance against his size and strength. She looked about the kitchen, hoping for some solution, finding nothing but emptiness and disappointment. Feeling his patient waiting, she sighed and turned back to face him.

"You could go across to the neighbor's and get water." She nodded toward Lother's place. "I'll stay here and tidy up a bit." If he got so much as halfway across the pasture, she'd figure out some way to bar the broken door.

Kody's eyes narrowed.

She crossed her arms over her chest as if she hoped to protect her thoughts from his piercing gaze.

The man looked at the empty bucket, gave a long, considering study of the useless pump, then stared across the pasture. "How long you been out of water?" he asked, his voice soft but knowing.

Again she shrugged. Her problems were no concern of his.

He nodded toward the path. "Why don't you go get some?"

Her stomach lurched toward her heart, making her swallow hard to control the way her fear mixed with nausea. She didn't want Lother to know she was alone and had waited until dark two nights ago to slip over. She reasoned she could fill a pail and hurry away without detection. But his dog set up a din fit to wake the dead. Charlotte had tried to calm him. "It's me. You know me." She'd kept her voice low, but the dog wouldn't let up. Coming around after dark was a strange occurrence, not acceptable to the dog's sense of guard duty.

Charlotte had been forced to retreat without water in order to avoid being confronted by Lother.

"How long you been here alone?"

She pressed her lips together and jutted out her chin.

Kody adjusted his black cowboy hat and leaned back on worn cowboy boots. His gray shirt, laced at the neck, had seen better days. His pants were equally shabby. "Why ain't you walked out of this place?" He shook his head. "I don't get it. You've got the guts to face me with an empty gun, yet you hide in this derelict house without water."

How dare he? "What gives you the right—"

"Lady, despite the color of my skin—"

Which, Charlotte thought, had nothing to do with this whole conversation.

He continued in the same vein. "And the uncertainty of my heritage—"

One certainty he'd overlooked: this was none of his business. "I don't recall asking for your help," she said.

"I've been raised to care about the welfare of others."

That stumped her. How could she argue with something she also believed?

He continued. "You're out of water. And you're alone. It just plain ain't safe for a woman to be alone with so many drifters around."

"My brother is sending for me to join him."

"So you're going to sit here and wait?"

Why did he goad her? His words edged past her patience, her faith that Harry would indeed send for her, and dug cruel, angry fingers into her spine. "No, I'm not waiting." Why had she sat here for a whole week expecting the Hendersons to deliver a message? She spun on her heel and marched back to the dusty bedroom, threw her few things into the old carpetbag Nellie had left in the closet and rolled up the little bit of bedding. She stomped from the room, paused and grabbed the rifle. Not much good to her, but she'd return it to Harry, and when she did, she'd let him feel the sharp edge of her tongue for leaving her in such a position. Of course, she wouldn't. She wouldn't risk making him regret opening his home to her.

Ignoring the crunch of dirt under her shoes, she hurried out the door, gave one goodbye glance over her shoulder at the interior of the house and headed down the road. There was nothing for her here and no reason to stay. Besides, surely the Hendersons had a message by now and simply hadn't had time to deliver it.

Kody trailed after her.

She paused to glower at him. "Why are you following me?"

"Just wondering where you're going."

"To the neighbor. They might have a message from my brother, though I fail to see how it's any of your concern."

"I'll see you to this neighbor. My ma would have my hide if I didn't make sure you were safe." He pushed his hat farther back on his head and nodded as if she'd agreed.

"I'm quite capable of looking after myself. I don't need you keeping an eye on me. Go away." She steamed down the road, dragging her bundles and the rifle.

"I'm going the same direction. Why don't you let me put your things on Sam?"

She stubbornly plowed onward. When he sighed and fell in step with her, she paused. "Seems a shame to be wasting your time. You might find a job if you hurry to town."

"I ain't leaving you until I know you're safe. Ma would have my—"

"She'd have your hide. So you said."

"Are you always so contrary?"

"I'm the most compliant of persons." Except right now. "Normally."

"So it's just me."

"Yup. Now why don't you get on your horse and ride away?" She had never been sharp with anyone in her life, but this man prodded her the wrong way. "Sorry for being rude," she mumbled.

"I'm used to it."

Although he said this in a mild way, his words stopped her in her tracks and she turned to stare at him. His dark eyes gave nothing away. Nor did his blank expression, but she understood he meant he faced unkind comments because of his race.

"Huh," she finally said, unwilling to point out that not everyone felt the same way. She couldn't say how she felt about the man, but it had nothing to do with his race and everything to do with the way he got under her skin like a long, unyielding sliver. She hurried on, not surprised when he walked beside her.

"How far to this neighbor?"

"The Hendersons. Three miles. Big Rock is a few miles farther." She hoped the suggestion he might like to hurry in that direction would be clear.

"Yup."

The weight of the bag made her shoulder ache. The bedroll kept slipping from her arms and the rifle banged against her shins, but she paid them scant attention. She was used to working hard without complaining.

Kody caught the bedroll just as it threatened to escape her grasp.

"That's mine," she protested.

"So it is." He tied it to the saddle and reached for the rifle.

"That's Harry's and I intend to see he gets it back."

"Harry would be your brother?"

"Of course."

"Well, when you give it back, I suggest you do it like this." He waved the gun as if hitting someone with it, then rubbed his head, moaning.

Despite the fact she didn't want Kody to tie her meager belongings to the saddle, despite the fact she didn't want him accompanying her, she laughed because his action so accurately echoed her sentiments. Though she would never do it. No. She'd hand the gun to him meekly and promise to work hard and not argue with Nellie. She'd done so over and over just to make sure Harry wouldn't send her away. Like he'd done when she was twelve. How grateful she'd been when he took her back. Only with Harry did she have a safe place.

Remembering sucked away the last drops of anger, so when Kody reached for the carpetbag, she handed it to him without argument. And submissively followed him down the road.

A few minutes later, Charlotte pointed to the low house. "The Hendersons'." They paused at the turnoff. She reached for her things. "Thank you for your company."

Kody touched the brim of his hat and gave a slight nod. "My pleasure."

She wondered if he mocked her. She shrugged. What did it matter? She marched to the door and knocked. Mr. Henderson opened. Mrs. Henderson stood at his shoulder, holding the new baby. "I've come to see if there's any word from Harry."

Two older people stood by, watching curiously. The three other children eyed Charlotte.

"No, nothing. I would have ridden over if I heard anything. Haven't been to town for a couple of days. Not since I picked up my folks. They've come to help."

"Perhaps I could wait here." She knew as soon as she spoke it wasn't possible. They must be crowded to the rafters already. "Never mind. I'll go to town and see if there's a message waiting." *Please, God, let there be some word.* Her silent prayer grew urgent. What would she do if there wasn't?

Chapter Three

Kody waited at the side of the road. He didn't really want to help her, but if he ever saw Ma again he wanted to be able to face her without any guilty deed to hide. She'd raised him to see and respond to the needs of others. He only wished others had been taught the same and saw past his heritage to his heart. But it no longer mattered. He had a destination—northern Canada. He'd heard a man could get cheap land without the uncertain benefit of neighbors. It sounded like his kind of place.

He settled back out of sight behind a low drift of soil and watched as Charlotte made her way to the door and knocked.

A young man and woman opened to her. Kody strained but couldn't make out any words until the man nodded. "Certainly there might be something by now. I'm sorry I can't take you."

Charlotte murmured a reply, then turned and plodded back to the road. "We can fill the canteen and clean up."

He handed it to her. "You go ahead. I'll wait here."

"I thought you were anxious to wash."

He studied the house, the door now closed. "Your friends won't understand your keeping company with me."

"I'm not keeping company with anyone."

He didn't make a move toward the nearby water trough.

"They do understand the need for water."

Sam whinnied and nudged Kody. He could ignore his own thirst, but it hardly seemed fair to deprive Sam of a drink. "Lead on," he murmured, a sense of exposure causing him to put the horse between him and the windows of the house.

They both washed, then Kody pumped fresh water for them to drink. He filled the canteen and waited as Sam drank his fill.

Charlotte wiped the back of her hand across her mouth and smoothed her damp hair off her face. "I'm going on to town. Harry must have sent word by now." She hitched the rifle over her shoulder, tried to tuck the unwieldy bedroll under one arm as she struggled to carry the bulky bag in the other. Then she resolutely headed down the road.

Knowing he had to do what Ma would consider the right thing, Kody fell in beside her. "How far is it, did you say?"

"Didn't." She paused. "Five miles."

He swallowed a groan. He wasn't used to walking and had already used his feet for three miles while Sam plodded along with an empty saddle. "Seems a shame for Sam to be doing nothing."

"No need for you to go out of your way."

"I hadn't planned on going to Big Rock. Hadn't not planned it, either. I'm only passing through on the way to something better. Picking up work where I can find it on my way north."

"What's up north?"

"Canada and a new life." As soon as he earned some more money he'd be ready to start over. "Hear you can find places where you never see another soul for months at a time."

"I'm here to tell you it can get might lonely not seeing another person." She shot him a look so full of disgust he chuckled.

He understood her response to being alone differed vastly from his own reasons for wanting it, so he didn't say anything.

They walked onward a few steps.

"Seems a shame for Sam to be doing nothing."

"No one asked you to accompany me. Get on and ride for Canada."

He snorted. "My ma would give me a real dressing-down if she heard I'd done such an ungentlemanly thing."

"Your ma isn't going to know, now is she?"

"You can never be sure." His voice rang with a mixture of regret and pride.

She laughed. The sound made his insides happy. "I've heard of mothers having eyes in the back of their heads," she said. "But this is the first time I heard someone suspect their mother of having long-distance sight."

He smiled, liking how it eased his mind. He'd gotten too used to scowling. "It ain't so much she'll see me do something, but if I ever see her again, she'll see it in my eyes." He'd never been able to fool Ma. She seemed to see clear through him. Which was one more reason to stay away from Favor, and Ma and Pa and all that lay in that direction.

Charlotte stopped and considered him. "Do you know how fortunate you are to have such a mother? If I had such a mother I'd never leave her. What are you doing going to Canada to be alone?"

"I have my reasons. Now save me from my mother's displeasure and ride Sam to town."

She studied him for a long moment. His skin tightened at the way she looked at him. He saw the fear and caution in her eyes, knew she saw him as a redskin, someone to avoid.

With a hitch of one shoulder to persuade the rifle to stay in place, she turned her steps back down the road.

He'd met this kind of resistance before and sighed loudly enough for her to pause. "My horse ain't Indian. Or half-breed."

Her shoulders pulled up inside her faded brown dress. He could practically see her vibrate, but didn't know if from anger or fear or something else. She let her bag droop to her feet and turned to face him. The sky lightened, with the brassy sun poking through the remnants of the dust storm, and he saw her eyes were light brown.

"Are you accusing me of prejudice?" she demanded, her voice soft, her eyes flashing with challenge as if daring him to think it, let alone say it.

Could she really be free of such? His heart reared and bucked as long-buried hopes and dreams came to life—acceptance, belonging, so many things. He shoved them away, barricaded them from his thoughts. Best he be remembering who he was, how others saw him. "Nope. Just stating a fact."

"I couldn't care less if your horse is Indian,

black, pink or stubborn as a mule. I prefer to walk." She spun around and marched down the road, sidling sideways to capture the escaping bedroll with her hip.

He grinned at her attempts to manage her belongings. For a moment he stared after her. She said words of acceptance, but he doubted she meant them as anything more than argumentative.

He followed, leading Sam. "He ain't stubborn."

"How nice for you." She continued, unconcerned by the wind tugging at her skirt and dragging her coppery-brown hair back from her forehead, undaunted by her belongings banging against her shins with every step.

Mule-headed woman. She made him want to prod at her more, see what would surface. He tried to think of a way to challenge her insistence on walking, wanting to somehow force her to state her opinion on his race. No doubt she had the same reservations as—ha, ha, good word choice. Again, his mother would have been amused. The same reservations about Indians most white folk. "My mother would want you to ride," he murmured.

Finally she nodded. "For your mother." He secured her things to the saddle, then she tucked her skirt around her legs and used his cupped hands to assist herself onto Sam's back. "I'll ride partway. You can ride the rest."

He didn't argue, but nothing under the brassy sun would allow him to ride while a white woman walked at his side. He could just imagine the comments if anyone saw them.

"Seems everyone wants a new life," she said from her perch on Sam's back. "Except me. I've been quite happy with the one God provided."

He wondered how being abandoned made her happy or caused her to think God had provided for her. "How long since your brother left?"

She darted him a look, then shifted her gaze to some distant point down the road. "Near a week."

Kody had learned to let insults roll off him without response. In fact, he'd learned to ignore lots of things in life. But a week? Well, he figured she had to be made of pretty strong stuff to still be fighting.

They walked on for the distance of half a mile until Charlotte broke the silence. "Why are you so anxious to go where you never see another soul?"

Kody didn't answer at first. Wasn't sure how to. This woman had a family. Sure, her brother had left her behind. Maybe with the best of intentions. But she expected him to welcome her into his new home. What would she know about how it felt to be a half-breed? How it affected everyone and everything in his world? How people expected him to be a wild Indian? At times his frustration made him want to act like one. "Sometimes a man likes to be alone."

"Don't you feel the need to have someone to talk to?"

Always. Try as he might, he never got used to keeping his thoughts inside himself. "Sam here is a good listener."

She laughed, a sound like water rippling over rocks. A sound trickling through his senses like someone brushing his insides with a feather. "If you want only listening you could park a rock on your saddle and talk to it. Seems to me a person wants a bit more. Someone to agree or argue. Someone to acknowledge your presence."

He refused to let her words poke at his loneliness. He'd made his decision. There was no looking back.

They fell into quiet contemplation as they continued toward the town. Kody's thoughts always seemed to have a mind of their own, and after talk about his mother, there was no way to keep himself from remembering her. She loved him. As did his father. He'd never doubted it. They treated him as their own and never once made him feel inferior. For that he loved them deeply, but life had created a solidly strong reason for him to move on. He stopped himself from thinking further along those lines. He'd made his decision and he wouldn't look back. Canada promised the sanctuary he sought. He hoped it would also provide forgetfulness of what he'd left behind.

Despite Charlotte's insistence she'd take her turn walking, Kody did not allow Sam to stop until Big Rock sat square in front of them. He pulled Sam off the road and helped Charlotte dismount. He hung back behind the low bushes at the side of the road. "You go on and see if Harry has sent you a message."

She brushed the dust off her dress and smoothed back her hair, which fell to her shoulders and trapped the golden rays of sunshine, then she took the bedroll and bag Kody handed her. He chuckled as she struggled to carry the rifle. "Might as well leave it behind."

She ignored his suggestion. "Thank you again and God bless you on your journey to Canada."

"You're welcome." He hunkered down behind the bushes and waited. He'd make his way into town later to assure himself she was okay, then he'd move on. He plucked a dry blade of grass and rolled it between his fingers. Used to be he could occupy his mind with such useless activity, but not today. His thoughts had been willful and troubling since he'd entered the house where Charlotte huddled alone. Something about her—her words of faith, her belief in family and belonging—

reminded him of what he'd left behind. He didn't thank her for bringing to his mind the very things he wanted to forget.

He turned to discuss the matter with Sam. "She thinks you're no better than a rock to talk to."

Sam snorted his disbelief.

"I know. I was offended, too. Shows what a woman knows. Sure, it's true you don't say much, but I know you understand."

Sam shook his head in agreement.

"Can't understand her brother abandoning her, though. She ain't so big she couldn't fit in somewhere."

Sam shook his head again.

"I sure hope the man has sent for her." He pushed to his feet and swung into the saddle. "Let's go see."

He pulled his hat low over his eyes and sat boldly upright, ready to face any challenge. He rode slowly through the wide streets of the suffering town, noted the vacant windows in several buildings. People pulled up and left everything behind as the drought and depression took their toll. A lone truck sat at the side of the street.

A man in the doorway of the feed store jerked to attention and watched Kody with narrowed eyes. Two old codgers leaned back on chairs in front of the mercantile. As Kody passed they crashed their chairs to all four legs. One spat on the sidewalk. Kody ignored them. He had no wish to start trouble. He only wanted to check on Charlotte and then he intended to head north as far as his empty stomach allowed before he tried to find some kind of work. It had become the pattern of his days. Sometimes, if the work was good or the pay promising, he stayed for days, even weeks. Other times, he earned a meal and moved on. Always north. Always toward his dream—Canada and forgetfulness. The journey had taken far longer than it should. He needed to make more effort to reach his goal.

He turned aside and stared at the display in the window of Johnson's General Store, though he only noted the post office sign. Charlotte would have gone inside to ask for her letter.

He waited, ignoring the stares from across the street. The two old men posed no threat, only annoyance and a reminder of what others saw when they looked at him.

Charlotte staggered out, a letter grasped in her hands. Her eyes had a faraway look as she stared past him, not seeing him, not, he guessed, seeing anything. At the shock on her face, he almost bolted off Sam, wanting to catch her before she stumbled and fell. Only the thunderous glance of a passing matron stopped him.

Charlotte collapsed on the nearby bench beside her belongings and shuddered.

Kody waited until the woman hurried on before he murmured, "You got your letter?" Seems she should have been a little more relieved to hear from her brother.

Slowly, as if it took all her mental energy, she pulled her gaze to him. She swallowed hard, her eyes seemed to focus and she shuddered again. "Harry says he's sorry, but they're still looking for a place. I'm to wait for further word from him. He suggested I stay with the Hendersons, but they're full with his parents there." Her eyes glazed. "I have no place to go."

The sound of someone on the sidewalk forced Kody to hold his tongue, though what could he tell her? Certainly she couldn't go back to the farm and no food or water, but she must have friends she could stay with for a few days.

A man stopped in front of Charlotte. "Well, if it isn't my neighbor. Haven't seen you in a few days, Charlotte. How are you doing?"

Charlotte folded the letter and tucked it into her bag. "I'm doing just fine, Lother. How about you?"

"A little lonely, my dear. But seeing you has fixed that right up."

Kody settled back, lowering his head and acting for all the world like he'd fallen asleep in the saddle. He didn't like the tone of proprietorship he heard in this Lother's voice, but it was none of his business and maybe the man would offer Charlotte the protection she needed.

Charlotte shuffled back, tucking her feet under the bench.

"What's this?" The man indicated the bedroll and carpetbag on the bench. "Planning a trip, are you?"

The storekeeper had moseyed out to take part in the conversation. "Harry and his wife moved out. Miss Charlotte's waiting for word to join them. That what your letter says?" he asked. "Harry sending for you?"

Charlotte shrank even farther back. She stared past Lother.

Kody lifted his chin just enough that their gazes connected. At the trapped look in her eyes he squeezed his hands into fists.

"No need for you to leave the country." Lother's words were low, his voice soft, yet Kody heard something he didn't like. The sort of noise a rattler made before it struck. "I'm willing to share my name and my home with you."

Charlotte's chin jutted out. "I have other plans."

"Joining your brother?" the storekeeper asked.

Charlotte flashed the man a defiant look. "That's my business, isn't it?"

"Mighty important business, too." The man snorted and returned inside.

Lother rocked back on his heels. "You're a strong young woman. 'Spect you could produce a whole lot of sons. Man needs sons to help on the farm. That brother of yours might be willing to sell me his land real cheap. Or I could wait a bit and get it for back taxes. With sons to help I could expand."

Kody wondered how soon he expected his sons to be big enough to help. Ma had taken in several babies while Kody lived at home, and he seemed to remember they were nothing but work for a couple of years and then they only ran around getting into mischief. Not much help, in his estimation. But this man had other plans for his babies. Plans including Charlotte as a broodmare. Kody twisted the reins until his hands hurt.

Lother touched Charlotte's cheek. "You'll do just fine," he said, his voice was as oily as the matted hair poking out from under the blackened edges of his hat. Kody could never understand a man who didn't wash up and comb his hair occasionally.

Charlotte twitched away from the man's touch, her eyes wide, dark with fear and something more, something Kody could only guess was loathing. It was plain she didn't much like this man.

Kody didn't like him at all.

Lother shoved Charlotte's belongings aside and sat very close, pushing his thigh against hers.

The man went too far. Kody leaned forward, preparing to spring to Charlotte's defense.

But Charlotte leaped to her feet. "Excuse me, I have to get to the train station." She grabbed her belongings and hurried down the street.

Lother called after her, "You best be changing your mind soon and stop playing Miss High-and-Mighty. Ain't like you got other beaux." The man turned, saw Kody watching him. "What are you staring at, Injun? Move along."

Kody didn't need the man's permission, nor did he swing Sam into the street because he'd been ordered to. He had to see what Charlotte had up her sleeve. She'd said her brother had told her to wait. Did she have somewhere to go? Someplace safe from this Lother man?

He rode slowly to the end of the block and circled around by a back street to the train station. He dismounted and shuffled slowly to the platform, acting as if he had no reason in the world to be there other than aimless boredom. He didn't want to attract attention, nor have anyone suspect he had any interest in Charlotte.

She sat on a bench in the shade, slumped over her knees as if in pain.

He controlled the urge to hurry to her side and, instead, sauntered along the platform to stand near the edge, facing the tracks. His back to her, he said, "You figure out a place to go?"

She sniffed, a dry, determined sound that brought a slight smile to his lips. He'd expected tears, not this attitude of defiance. "I have no money. No family apart from Harry. No one here has room or ability to keep me. But I'm not stuck, if that's what you're thinking. I'm not alone. God is with me. He's promised to provide all I need. I'm sitting here praying."

"Waiting for a miracle?" Far as he could see, God had not smiled any more favorably on this woman than on himself. For his part, he'd given up waiting for miracles or, for that matter, evidence of God's love.

"I guess you don't believe in miracles or God's provision."

He crossed his arms over his chest and stared down the empty tracks. "Can't say one way or the other. Might be God sends them both your way."

"I'm counting on it."

There seemed nothing more to say after that. He could, having done his duty, ride away and leave her to God's care. Yet he didn't move. How often had he heard Ma say, "Son, what kind of people are we if we see a soul in need and turn our backs?

Whatever the color of your skin, that uncaring attitude is savage." He wished he could shut off her voice, but it spoke softly in the back of his mind. She practiced what she preached, always helping those in need often without so much as a word of thanks. "I don't do it for the praise of men," she'd say. "I do it for God. He sees and knows my heart."

Kody had not one doubt what his mother would do in this situation. And what she would expect him to do. But she saw it in terms of black and white. He saw it in shades of red. He smiled, knowing Ma would appreciate the irony of his thoughts.

He uncurled his arms and let his fists hang at his sides. He could not walk away from his training. Again, he smiled, seeing the incongruity of his reasoning—unable to walk away from his training, yet determinedly riding away from his parents who had provided the training. His smile flattened. Best for those back home that he headed north, far, far from them all.

Except if he was to do what Ma expected, that might change. "I know someplace where you can stay safely until you get word from your brother."

"You do?"

"With my mother and father." It totally fouled his plans, but he could not leave Charlotte here.

He heard her huff. Knew she would refuse.

"You got a better idea?"

"Yes. I'll wait back at the farm."

He spun around to face her. "You can't mean that. You have no water. No food."

Her stubborn look didn't change.

"And what about your friend Lother?"

"He's not my friend." She looked down the street as if fearing the man would follow her. Slowly, she brought her gaze back to Kody and stared at him for a full thirty seconds. "Seems I don't have a whole lot of choices."

He could hardly describe her reaction as grateful. "Maybe it's the miracle you've prayed for." He knew from the scowl on her lips that she didn't believe it any more than he did. "I need to get a few things. Why don't you go back to the store and arrange to have any messages forwarded care of Reverend Douglas in Favor, South Dakota?"

She nodded, reluctantly, he figured, and he left her to take care of that detail while he headed toward the livery barn. He patted his pocket, knowing his purse would be much lighter before he left town.

This decision of his meant he would be heading south, instead of north, heading back to the very place he'd vowed to leave behind forever.

Chapter Four

It took all Charlotte's self-control to keep from wailing with frustration and fear. A miracle? An answer to prayer? It certainly wasn't either in her estimation. She'd prayed for rescue, someone to offer her a home. The only person to do so was a half-breed. And Lother. She shuddered. She'd as soon sit on the step of Harry's empty house and wait to die of thirst as marry that man. Of the two, Kody seemed slightly less undesirable. At least he only wanted to escort her to his parents'. Or so he said. *God, I know You can't plan for me to ride out with this man. Please send someone else before he returns.*

Why couldn't some young mother needing help come along and see her? She'd willingly care for babies in exchange for a safe place to live. Or why couldn't an older couple shuffle by, the woman all crippled up and in pain and needing someone to run and fetch for her? Charlotte would put up with any amount of crankiness if it meant a roof over her head. Hadn't she been doing so for years, catering to Nellie's demands? And for what? To be thrown out or left behind at the slightest whim? God was in control. She knew that, but sometimes she found it hard to see how things could work out for good. But wasn't that when trust came in? When she couldn't comprehend circumstances?

Wait on the Lord. Wait and see His deliverance. She wished she could read the Bible and find appropriate words of comfort, but Harry had taken it with him.

She sat, waiting expectantly, until her skin began to twitch.

But the platform remained empty. So she trudged back to the store and made arrangements for the mail. Every step carried a prayer for God to intervene. No miracle occurred on her way to the store or her way back, and she resumed her position on the bench, pleading with God to do something. Surely there were people who would welcome her help in exchange for a warm corner to sleep in.

"Psst." The soft noise pulled her attention to the far end of the station, to a small cluster of trees where Kody waited. "Let's get out of here."

She didn't want to get out; she wanted to stay. She held her breath, praying for God to provide in the next two seconds something—someone—posing less risk than the man waiting for her.

Nothing.

Seems God had narrowed her choice down to this one option. Perhaps she'd displeased God, too, and He chose to ignore her. She pushed to her feet, taking her time about gathering her things, waiting for God to bestow better, praying with every breath. *God, help me. I trust You, even though things don't look good right now.*

Slowly she crossed the platform, her shoes thudding hollowly on the worn wood, the dusty air catching at her throat. She paused to glance in the window, saw Mr. Sears at the wicket. He looked up, saw her and turned away dismissively.

"Hurry," Kody whispered.

The way he glanced about him sent warning skitters along the surface of her skin. "Why?" She spoke the word aloud, albeit softly.

"You're a white woman, I'm a half-breed. Need I say more?"

Caught up in his suspicions, she glanced over her shoulder to make sure no one saw her and then picked up her pace.

Kody took Harry's rifle, her bedroll and carpetbag—all her worldly possessions—and hung them neatly from the saddle, then helped her onto the old black mare he'd found somewhere.

Her doubts intensified. What did she know about this man apart from his own words? "Where'd you get the horse?"

He crossed his arms over his chest and stared up at her, his eyes hidden under the rim of his hat. "You figure I stole her?"

Her ears stung with heat that her caution had sounded accusing. She averted her gaze. "Just asking."

Kody grunted. "It might ease your mind to know I bought her fair and square from the livery barn. The owner seemed quite willing to part with her. He's running low on feed."

At his words a release of tension left Charlotte's spine weak. She didn't care to think the law would be after them.

Charlotte studied her mount—thin and probably as hungry as she was. She patted the mare's neck soothingly.

Kody pulled out of the trees and into the street, drew back as a truck putt-putted past, then flicked the reins and continued.

Charlotte started to follow, but when he headed away from the town to the north, her heart kicked in alarm. Did he expect her to follow him to Canada without protest? She pulled on the reins and turned the mare down Main Street. "Favor is to the south," she muttered.

Kody kicked Sam in the ribs and bolted to her side. "You can't ride through town."

"Why not? I'm a free woman. I've broken no laws."

He reached for her reins, but she jerked away from him.

"Again, I remind you, you're a white woman, I'm a—"

"So you said. But I am not riding north with you."

Kody grunted and fell back to her horse's rear. He pulled his hat lower over his face. "You're going to regret this," he murmured as he followed.

Charlotte kept her thoughts to herself, but she didn't intend to regret riding north when relief lay to the south, nor did she intend to ride out without giving God one more chance to send an alternative to riding into the unknown with a dark stranger.

As they traveled the three-block length of the street, Mrs. Williams stepped into view. The woman cleaned and cooked for Pastor Jones. Surely this was God's answer. The good Mrs. Williams would offer sanctuary to a stranded young woman. Charlotte edged her horse closer to the sidewalk and called out a greeting.

"Charlotte, how are you doing?"

"I'm actually in need of shelter. Harry has moved and until he sends for me, I am homeless. Perhaps you'll allow me to stay with you. I could find a job and provide for myself. I just need a place to sleep."

"I don't see how you could find work when hundreds of men are unemployed, and besides, with my husband being sick…" The older woman shook her head. "I'm sorry."

Charlotte nodded. "Thank you, anyway." She edged the horse back into the street, muttering to herself, "I wouldn't be in her way at all."

Kody grunted. "Times are hard."

Right then, Lother stepped out of the hotel. Charlotte shuddered as Lother glanced past her to Kody.

"You. Injun. What are you doing following my woman? Leave her alone." He waved his arms like he shooed chickens into the henhouse.

Kody didn't answer but said softly to Charlotte, "Make up your mind. Either ride on or stay with him."

"Some choice." She nudged her plodding horse onward, ignoring Lother's words following her down the street.

"No decent woman would keep company with an Injun of her own will." Anything more he had to say was lost in the clatter of horses' hooves.

Mrs. Craven peeked out her window as they

passed, her eyes narrowing on Kody, then widening at Charlotte's riding with him. But she let the curtain drop without offering help.

As they rode out of town, Charlotte swallowed back the bitterness rising in her throat and resisted an urge to shake the dust from her skirts. She only asked for a little shelter. Instead, she was forced to accept the charity and kindness of a stranger. She prayed kindness guided this man's actions. *God, I need help. Please send someone.*

A mile down the road, Kody edged forward to ride at her side, but neither of them spoke. What could she possibly say? She'd accepted his help out of desperation. She felt no gratitude. Only a mile-wide hope that God would still see fit to send an alternative to accompanying this man into the unknown.

They had ridden perhaps an hour when the sound of an approaching car brought them to a stop at the side of the road. Charlotte expected the car to growl past and turned her head to avoid the cloud of dust. But the vehicle drew to a halt beside them and Sheriff Mack stepped out.

She wanted to laugh and cry and cheer all at once. God hadn't forgotten her. Why hadn't it occurred to her to consult the sheriff? "Sheriff, am I glad to see you. Perhaps you can help me."

"That's why I'm here." He pulled out his gun

and leveled it at Kody. "Put your hands in the air and get down real slow."

For the second time in the same afternoon, Kody's arms went up and he dropped to the ground easily and gracefully.

Charlotte's heart stalled with alarm. Had she unwittingly accompanied a fugitive? She swallowed hard, trying to ease the gritty feeling inside, like she'd taken in too much dust in the last blow.

What had Kody done?

And why had she allowed herself to believe he wanted to help her? She'd been duped by talk about a God-fearing mother. She'd been taught you couldn't judge a man by the color of his skin. Seems you couldn't judge by his words or demeanor, either.

"Something wrong, Sheriff?" Kody asked in a low voice, apparently unconcerned.

She doubted he could be as indifferent as he appeared with the sheriff motioning him away from his horse.

"Charlotte, get in the car," Sheriff Mack said. "And you—" he kept his gun steady as he approached Kody "—turn around slow."

Charlotte sighed in relief as she got into the front seat of the sheriff's car. Sheriff Mack lived with his maiden sister. They'd be glad to take her in and she'd find a way to prove her value to them.

She watched as the sheriff handcuffed Kody and pushed him into the backseat. *I wonder what he's done. Too bad. He seemed like a nice enough fellow.*

The sheriff grabbed up the horses and tied them to the car. "Good thing Lother sent me after you," he said to Charlotte as he got behind the wheel.

A prickly sensation crawled along Charlotte's skin. She pulled her skirt down hard and tucked it around her legs. "Lother? What's he got to do with this?"

The sheriff chuckled. "No need to play coy with me, Charlotte. He told me you two were to marry. Said he saw this Indian take you out of town." Sheriff Mack started the car and edged down the road toward Big Rock. "But don't you worry. I'll take care of your kidnapper." He scowled over his shoulder at Kody. "Guess you know better than to expect any mercy. It's the rope for you." He turned and smiled at Charlotte. "I'll make sure you're safe with Lother before nightfall. Might even agree to stand up for him at his wedding." He nodded, seeming pleased with himself.

Charlotte stared at the sheriff. Nothing he said made any sense. Safe with Lother? She shuddered. "Are you saying Lother thinks I've been kidnapped?"

"Good thing he saw your predicament."

"But I went of my own free will."

The sheriff stopped the car and faced her. "Didn't you just ask me for help?"

"I need someplace to stay until Harry sends for me." Her eyes stung with embarrassment as she prepared to beg. "I thought I could stay with you and your sister." She hated the desperate tone of her voice, but truth was, she had quickly dispensed with her pride about the time she walked off the train platform. "I could scrub up after the prisoners for you."

Sheriff Mack shook his head. "No can do. If I take you back, I'll turn you over to Lother. It's my duty." He patted Charlotte's hand. "Now don't you fret none. Many a young lady has been nervous on her wedding day. It's perfectly normal. But once it's done, you'll feel better."

Anger and disgust raged inside her at the way these men decided her future with absolutely no regard for her wishes. "I would not marry Lother if he was the last man on earth." She tipped her head toward Kody. "This man is the only one who has had the decency to offer to help."

Sheriff Mack looked uncomfortable. "Now, Miss Charlotte, no need to get all high and mighty on me."

"He's done nothing wrong. Release him at once."

"Now wait one cotton-pickin' minute."

"Now." She tilted her head toward Kody, indicating she wanted him released.

"You're making a mighty big mistake."

But Charlotte would not relent.

Muttering dark predictions about her future, Sheriff Mack took the handcuffs off Kody. "You're free to go."

Charlotte stepped out of the car as Kody backed away. He remained motionless as Sheriff Mack untied the horses. When Kody made no move to take the reins, Charlotte reached for them.

Sheriff Mack looked at her a moment, then scrunched up his lips on one side and made a sound of disgust. "Lother isn't going to be happy about this."

She didn't answer, although her brain burned with angry retorts. *Too bad about Lother. That's your problem, not mine. Next time you should…* There would be no next time for her. She intended to seek refuge with Kody's parents in Favor. What choice did she have? No one else offered sanctuary. *God, help me.*

She turned her head away as the dust whipped up around the departing vehicle.

Only after the gray cloud abated did Kody turn and in one smooth move, leap onto Sam's back. "Let's get out of here," he muttered as he urged Sam into a run.

Charlotte climbed onto the mare's back and kicked her sides, trying to catch Kody, but it seemed the mare's fastest pace was a bone-shuddering trot that practically shook Charlotte from her back. After several futile attempts to get the animal to gallop, Charlotte settled back into a slow walk as Kody and Sam disappeared over a hill. The puffs of dust swirling from Sam's hooves gave her direction.

Why would no one help her? *I wouldn't be a burden. I'd make them glad they'd taken me in.* But her silent arguments were a waste of time. She had to think about the future. *My times are in Your hands.* God had promised. He would not fail her.

With each exhalation she let out fear and disappointment. With every indrawn breath, she pulled assurance and peace into her heart. Certainly she couldn't understand why He would choose to send help in the form of a stranger and a half-breed. But she would not fear. She would trust. She'd allow Kody to take her to his parents, but she'd be on guard at all times to make sure she got there safely.

Courage and determination returned before she caught up to him twenty minutes later.

He lounged in the shade of a ragged rock, his legs outstretched, his head tipped back and his hat pulled over his eyes.

She dismounted, swaying a little with light-headedness.

"Not used to riding?" Kody murmured.

How could he see with his hat pulled down? "I ride fine." It wasn't riding that made her weak but lack of food. Yesterday she'd eaten the last dry biscuit.

He sat up so quickly she jerked back, alarm skittering across the surface of her skin, eliciting goose bumps. She grabbed the saddle horn, preparing to mount up again and ride away if he threatened her. She sighed with defeat. He could probably outrun the mare on foot. She would have to find another way of protecting herself. Her mind blanked, her blood pooled in a cold puddle in the pit of her stomach as she admitted her defenselessness. In the middle of open country. In the company of a stranger. *God is with me. I will not fear.* Despite her assurance of God's protection, her mouth remained dry.

But Kody only pushed his hat back to study her.

She took a good hard look at him, hoping for something to ease her fears. Eyes blacker than coal. No surprise. Skin bronzed. Again, no surprise. But the kind gleam in his eyes caught her off guard. One thing her mother had said repeatedly before her death, "Charlotte, never judge a man by his looks. Always seek below the surface." Of course, even the look in his eyes revealed nothing of what lay beneath. Nevertheless, it eased her fear.

"You could have changed your mind back there."

She shuddered. "And go to Lother? I'd sooner be tied out in the sun and left to bake."

Kody's black eyes bored into her gaze.

The skin on her cheeks tightened as she realized she'd blurted out one of the ways Indians supposedly used to torture captives.

He nodded. "So be it." He strode over to Sam and dug into one of his packs.

Relieved to be free of his intense look, Charlotte sucked in the hot, dusty air and coughed.

"Here." He handed her a canteen. "It will have to last us the day, so ration yourself."

"Thank you." She tipped her head back and let the water fill her mouth, kept it there, savoring the relief to her parched tongue and throat before she swallowed. She allowed herself one more mouthful, then screwed the top back on and held the canteen toward Kody.

"It's yours. Hang it from your saddle."

"Thanks."

"Hold out your hand."

She hesitated as a spidery sensation crept up her spine. Was he trying to trick her? Take advantage of her?

"Look, you're going to have to trust me."

Trust him? No. She couldn't even trust her brother, her only living relative. She wasn't sure she would ever trust anyone again. Except God, of course.

Kody made an impatient sound. "Take it or leave it." He began to withdraw his hand.

She realized she'd made him angry and understood it made her even more vulnerable, so she opened her palm to him, keeping a careful distance between their hands.

Raisins dribbled into her hand.

Raisins? She'd expected… She didn't know what, but not this. Why had God chosen such an unusual way to satisfy her hunger? Her mouth watered in anticipation of the waiting treat and she decided to deal with her hunger first and her questions later.

"Thank you." Her voice rose in a squeak.

He grunted acknowledgment and swung up on Sam. "Best keep moving."

As Charlotte nibbled the raisins, savoring them one at a time, her thoughts returned to doubts about her decision. She blinked back tears. It wasn't her fault she'd been left with little choice but to ride across the country with a stranger. But who was she to blame? Lother? Now that he knew her to be alone, she would never be safe back at the farm. No one in Big Rock offered her shelter. Did they not believe in Christian charity? And what about Harry? He had promised to care for her always. Of course, he hadn't stopped caring. Things just hadn't panned out yet. They'd soon be together again as they should be. Perhaps she should blame Nellie with her whining and complaining. The last few weeks, it seemed no matter how hard she tried, Charlotte could not please her sister-in-law. But then many people, men and woman alike, found the continued drought more than they could bear. The drought? Surely that accounted for some of her problems? But who sent the rains or withheld them? God. Ultimately blaming anyone meant blaming God and she couldn't do that. She trusted Him, depended on His continuing care to see her safely returned to Harry's home. Relieved to have settled the matter, she glanced about her, seeing vaguely familiar landmarks. "We'll never make Favor by nightfall."

"Nope."

She glanced at him. He seemed unconcerned, but then, he was probably used to sleeping on the trail. The very thought filled her with fresh alarm. "Where will we spend the night?"

"With friends of mine." Kody slowed Sam so he could ride at her side. "Seems you have no choice but to accept hospitality where you can find it."

He'd pinpointed her hard feelings. She had no choice. She'd had none when her mother died and Harry became her sole guardian. She'd had none when Harry sent her to the Applebys, nor when he left her behind a few days ago. She had little choice now. She suddenly laughed. She didn't need to trust people to help her. "God will take care of me wherever we spend the night."

He turned in his saddle to give her a hard look. "Seems you're depending on me to help do God's work. Does that make me an instrument of God's using?" He paused but before she could answer, he continued, "Or does it make me an accidental encounter?"

She wondered if he mocked her faith. Or were his questions sincere? "Do you have cause to wonder which you are?"

"You better believe I have."

"And what would it be, if you don't mind my asking?"

Kody brought Sam to a stop and turned to stare at her.

Charlotte decided he looked surprised and disbelieving at the same time.

He rolled up his sleeve and pointed to his arm. "I'm sure you've noticed the color of my skin." He tugged at one braid. "And the color of my hair."

Indeed she had. And yes, she shrank back,

knowing his heritage, but she trusted God to keep her safe. And whether or not He used a half-breed to serve His purposes, she would continue to trust Him. Besides, did God care about the color of a man's skin?

She turned to look Kody full in the face. "Doesn't the Scripture say there is no difference between people?"

"Words mean nothing to most people." He jerked forward and resumed their journey.

The sun beat down with unrelenting persistence. An hour or so later, Kody pulled off the road into the meager shelter of some trees. "We'll let the horses rest out of the sun for a while."

Charlotte kept her gaze on the trail ahead. She'd prefer to keep moving, the sooner to reach safety, but she understood the wisdom of giving the horses a break from the heat.

He settled down in the shade of a tree and pulled his hat over his face.

Slowly, Charlotte got down from her horse. She found a tree as far from Kody as she could and sank to the heated ground, trying unsuccessfully to pull both shoulders into the shade. The blazing sun sucked oxygen from the air. Lethargy seeped into her bones. She blinked, trying to keep her eyes open, knowing she'd be easy prey if she allowed herself to fall asleep. But sleep continued to threaten. Unwilling to succumb, she pushed to her feet and moved around slowly to keep herself awake. She leaned against a tree and stared across the parched fields.

"Get up real slow." A rough voice spoke behind her.

Charlotte stiffened and sucked in a gulp of oven-hot air. Slowly she turned. She couldn't see the speaker and edged a little to the right to see past the mare grazing placidly between her and Kody. What she saw made her blood jolt to her heart in a pounding pulse—two men, unshaven and unkempt, looking as appealing as last week's slop. One aimed a small handgun at Kody.

Kody folded his legs under him and rose in one slow movement.

"Hands above your head and don't try no funny stuff."

The shorter man, a menacing sneer slashing his face, held the gun. The taller man had a narrow face and beady eyes, reminding Charlotte of a rat. She pushed her fears to one side and tried to think what she should do.

"Looks like a good pair of boots. Them and the horses will come in mighty handy, don't ya think, Shorty?"

Charlotte sent up a prayer for help and then her brain kicked into gear. It seemed they hadn't noticed her. If she kept quiet, maybe they wouldn't. She glanced around, saw a boulder several feet away. If she hid behind it and didn't make a sound…

But what would happen to Kody? He'd been kind enough to rescue her. So far, he'd been nothing but a gentleman. She had lingering doubts about her safety with him, but she had no such doubts about these two. She would *not* be safe with them. And she couldn't imagine they'd have any compunction about killing Kody. She could run and hide, or—she gulped—she could do something to help. She fought the fear racing up her limbs and setting her teeth to chattering and made up her mind. *God, help me.*

Silently, as slow as a shadow following the sun, crouching low, she moved away from the shelter of the tree and edged toward the mare. She reached the horse just as Kody pulled off his first boot, and she cautiously removed Harry's rifle. Thankfully the placid mare paid no attention to her.

Charlotte put the rifle to her shoulder and tried to think how to be more convincing with this pair than she had been with Kody. She took a deep breath to stop the gun from wavering in her hands, forced a deep scowl to her face. She feared her eyes were wide with fright and concentrated on narrowing them. Only then did she step out from behind the mare.

"Drop your gun." She did her best to sound menacing. In truth, she was surprised any words escaped. It felt as if someone had tried to padlock her throat shut.

They stared at her in disbelief. "Where'd you come from?"

"God sent me."

The pair glanced heavenward and shuffled backward like they feared the wrath of God. She smiled at their frightened look and jerked the rifle upward slightly in what she hoped was a scary gesture. "Drop the gun."

"Do as she says," Ratface said.

"I am." Shorty tossed the gun aside.

Kody dived for it and turned it on the pair. "Best be on your way," he said.

Lifting their feet high as if afraid they might step on something, the two beat it down the road, glancing over their shoulders every few steps to see if anyone—or perhaps anything—followed them.

Charlotte moved to Kody's side and they kept both guns aimed toward the fleeing men until they disappeared from sight.

Only then did Charlotte let the heavy rifle drop. She leaned over and gasped for air.

Kody laughed. It started as a little burst of what Charlotte took for relief, then grew steadily to a deep belly laugh.

She shot him a look of disbelief. She saw no humor in the situation. They'd just been threatened by two men who surely would have had taken more than their belongings. She shuddered to think of what they might have done to her. And Kody. Surely he'd been aware of the danger. How could he laugh?

Kody sobered as she scowled at him, although his eyes continued to brim with amusement and his smile seemed as wide as a door. "They really thought you dropped out of heaven. Scared them good. And to think that old rifle has no ammo." He chuckled some more. "Apart from your bravado."

"I fail to see what's so funny." She pulled herself onto the mare's back. "I intend to ride as far and as fast from those two as I can."

Kody leaped to Sam's back. "Did you see the look on their faces as they ran off? As if they expected a whole flock of avenging angels to descend?" He laughed again.

Charlotte tried to urge the mare into a gallop. She only wanted a safe place with no more threatening men. No more wondering what lay around the next corner. But the mare had one gait and would not be pushed. Charlotte sighed and stopped fighting the horse.

Kody stayed at her side as if a short halter rope connected the two horses. His continued chuckling annoyed her almost as much as did the fact that she felt safer with him there.

"You saved us."

He tried, she guessed, to persuade her to see the humor in something she found too frightening to be amusing. "God saved us. I prayed. He answered. It's that simple."

"Didn't see God holding the empty rifle. Only saw you, though I'm thinking those two drifters saw more."

She turned to study him. Saw he teased, but his words had triggered an idea. "Maybe they did see something more. Maybe God sent angels to surround us and only those two men saw them. Like that story in the Bible." The idea made her feel better and she smiled.

"Could be your miracle." He grinned at her.

"I believe it is." For a moment she let herself forget she'd only just met this man and let her heart open a crack to enjoy a shared laugh.

But just for a moment. She hadn't forgotten her precarious state—riding across the dried-out prairie with a stranger, confronting dangers on the trail, facing a fearful, uncertain future. It provided little reason for amusement.

They rode on, for the most part in silence. The lonely days of worry, too little food, too little water and now a long ride took their toll. Charlotte grew weary, barely able to stay awake. She swayed in the saddle.

Kody grabbed her shoulder to stop her from falling. "Hang on. Just a little farther."

She could barely keep her eyes open. Her head kept falling to her chest. Kody stayed close to her side, steadying her several times.

"We're here," Kody said.

She realized they'd stopped at a picket fence before a low white house. "Where's here?" Her words felt stiff on her tongue.

"Where we will spend the night."

A robust-looking woman opened the door, drying her hands on a towel. "Claude, we have visitors." She shaded her eyes and studied Kody and Charlotte. A tall man joined her at the doorway.

Suddenly the woman's face broke into a huge smile. "Well, I'll be. It's Kody Douglas." She rushed down the pathway.

Charlotte saw it in fractured glimpses through eyelids refusing to open more than a crack. She felt Kody jump to the ground, felt his steadying hands on her arm as he introduced his friends as Ethel and Claude. She tried to remember how to dismount, but her limbs refused to obey her brain.

Kody lifted her from the saddle and eased her to her feet. When her legs buckled, he scooped her into his arms and headed for the door.

"I can walk."

"No so good right now,"

"Put me down." Her protest was limp. "I need to get my things."

"I'll get them."

She didn't want to be a bother. She knew how people resented it.

"Stop fighting and let someone do for you for a change.

She ceased her weak struggles. He didn't sound annoyed at having to "do" for her. His arms tightened around her as he stepped over the threshold. He lowered her into a chair, pausing to murmur, "You saved my life. I guess that means I'm allowed to do things for you."

She opened her eyes and stared at him.

He hovered at her side, making sure she wasn't going to tip over, then slowly straightened, his dark gaze never leaving her face. She couldn't break away from his look.

"I'll get you something to drink and arrange for our accommodation."

She hadn't done anything to earn his favor except point a useless gun at two cowardly men and trust God to do the rest. But this appreciation, this attentive care to her needs, caught her off guard. The way it made her feel valued snuck right past her anger and fear, sidestepped the feeling she must make herself useful and settled down beside her heart like it meant to stay.

But it couldn't be.

She rested her elbows on the table and held her chin in her upturned palms, and despite the sluggishness of her sleep-hungry brain, she faced the hard, undeniable truth. Kody said he knew who he was—a half-breed. And she knew well who she was—a charity case who must prove her worth to keep from being tossed out on her ear.

It had been much too easy for Harry to leave her behind. She'd been getting complacent. Not working as hard as she should. When she rejoined them she would work doubly hard to make sure she had a place to live.

Chapter Five

The following afternoon, Kody reined Sam in at the fork in the road. If he kept pushing they could reach Favor before nightfall.

He glanced down the narrower road. Four years ago he'd said his final goodbye to what lay down there, promising himself and others he would never return. But all his noble intentions were powerless to stop him from turning aside, away from town and in the wrong direction.

Charlotte followed meekly. He already noticed she automatically did as told. In fact, she practically leaped to comply with the barest suggestion and she seemed to think she had to help with every chore. This morning she'd insisted on saddling her own horse.

He laughed, remembering how the saddle kept rolling under the mare's belly.

"What's so funny?" she demanded.

"Just thinking."

"Huh." She sounded suspicious.

Could be because he often and unexpectedly laughed as he recalled some of her little exploits. Like chasing off those two scoundrels yesterday. Just recollecting that made him laugh again. Come to think of it, he'd laughed more in the past two days than in the past two years. Or longer. Only two days ago he'd settled low in his saddle, with nothing on his mind but getting to Canada. Now his whole life had turned around.

He sobered. The sooner he returned to his original plans, the better. But seeing as he'd come this far, he might as well take one more detour. Somewhere deep inside his brain, a mocking voice called, *You're only making excuses and mighty glad you are of them, too.*

"You're laughing at me again, I suppose." She didn't sound overjoyed.

Glad of the diversion from his unwanted thoughts, his grin returned. "I gotta admit it was a lot of fun watching you try and saddle that old thing you're riding."

"I could've figured it out myself if you'd given me a chance."

He chuckled softly. "Thought you were anxious to get to Favor."

"You know I am now I have no choice, but I only came along with you because you pushed me to."

He snorted. What a stubborn woman. Several times she'd blamed him for making her leave that dried-out old house. "Don't I recall you stomping off down the road ahead of me?"

"Only 'cause you made it plain you planned to be a pain in the neck if I tried to stay."

He glanced over. She gave him a look full of balky defiance.

He laughed. "You and that mare make a good pair."

She blinked with surprise and then narrowed her eyes. "What's that supposed to mean?"

"That old mare picks her own pace and ain't about to let anyone convince her to change it. Seems you do same."

They plodded on. Sam had stopped trying to pick up the pace, accepting the mare's slower one. Kody itched to ride faster. The sooner he delivered Charlotte to his parents, the sooner he would turn around and head north.

Yeah? So why are you riding down this trail?

Did God have a hand in bringing him back?

"You implying I'm slow?"

"No, ma'am, not in the least." He restrained the laughter tickling his throat and turned to grin at her.

She gave him a look fit to slice bread. "You can stop staring now. I know you're meaning I'm stubborn. But you're wrong. I'm not stubborn. In fact, quite the opposite."

He shook his head. "Can't think what's the opposite of stubborn. Compliant?"

"Submissive." She spoke matter-of-factly. "Why are we riding this direction? I thought Favor lay down the other road."

He'd wondered how long it would take her to voice an objection. Seemed she could only shake the compliant attitude when pushed and pushed hard. And going the wrong direction was a hard push.

"We'll stay with friends of mine tonight. Safer than being on the road after dark. 'Course if not for that stubborn thing under you, we might have a chance of getting to Favor before nightfall. But…" He shrugged.

Charlotte patted the mare's neck. "She's faithful and gentle. Seems she should get a little credit for that."

Kody wondered if she thought the same of herself. He didn't know this Harry fellow and didn't want to. Far as he was concerned any man who rode off and left his sister to manage on her own ranked lower than worm juice. They'd talked some as they rode. When he learned she was only eighteen, he teased her about being young.

Upon getting him to confess to being twenty-one, she laughed. "Indeed, you are so aged."

He hadn't told her he felt too old for his years and yet not wise enough. He held on to the hope Canada would give him the distance to deal with both problems.

His destination lay around the next bend in the road. He reined in his horse and lounged in the saddle as if he had nothing better to do than stare out at the rolling hills. Toward Favor they would enter the irrigated area, which made the town prosperous even in the drought. A dam built earlier in the century ensured good crops. "You can always find work in the hills," people said, meaning both the irrigated flats and the hills surrounding the town, which supported a brick factory and a sugar-beet factory. Ranchers struggled a bit because of the low price for beef, but the hills with their copses of trees provided decent enough grazing.

"What are you waiting for?" Charlotte asked.

"Just looking around."

She settled back, uttering not one word of complaint, which didn't surprise him. She had not complained once about the discomforts of the trail even though she'd hardly been able to walk when they stopped for a noon break.

He supposed he should prepare her for what lay ahead. "My friends, who we'll spend the night with, are Indians, the Eaglefeathers. They live on a reservation."

She nodded. "Do they like it?"

He blinked. He'd expected protest, or hastily disguised shock. "Like what?"

"Living on the reservation."

"They don't have much choice."

"No choice about living there, maybe. But don't they have a choice about whether or not they like it?"

He had the feeling she wasn't just curious about his friends. More like exploring how other people dealt with events in their lives helped her find a way to deal with hers. And thinking that made him want to prod her. Force her to look at her own situation with both eyes wide-open, rather than through the filter of how others reacted.

"I think they have decided to make the best of it. Which doesn't mean they are sitting around waiting for life to happen to them."

He saw a flash of acknowledgment in her eyes and knew his words struck pay dirt.

"Is that what you think I'm doing? Sitting around waiting for something to happen?" Her soft words gave away little of her feelings, though he wondered if she could be as unaffected as she tried to appear. She hadn't been quick enough to stop the little gasp of surprise when she realized what he meant.

"You were just sitting in that empty house."

"I'm not anymore."

"Nope. But I get the feeling you're only planning to move the place where you sit and wait for Harry to invite you back into his family."

She looked away, letting her gaze follow the distant hills. "Sometimes the alternatives aren't too appealing."

He thought of Lother and had to agree.

She clucked the old mare into slow-motion forward. "Let's go."

He hesitated. He should probably have said more about where they were going. But then, what could he say? Some things could not be shared. Or admitted. No one must know his secret.

He should call her back. Return to the main road. Forget this little side trip. But he could not deny himself the chance to see how things were. He knew they would be fine, but once he saw, he could ride north again with a clear conscience.

Finally he reined in Sam behind Charlotte and the plodding mare.

From this direction, they reached the Eagle-feather home before the other homes on the reservation.

The low shack looked weary and worn since he'd last seen it, the unpainted wood weathered to gray. One lone, spindly tree struggled to survive beside the house. Two boxes sat against one wall. Kody knew they served as stools. A skitter of dust crossed the bare yard. The yard would have been swept that morning, every morning, in fact. A fire pit glowed in the center of the yard. He shifted his gaze away from the meager living quarters, but what he saw farther along didn't ease his sense that the Eaglefeathers, like many on reservations, struggled to eke out an existence. A thin horse stood in a tiny corral. A small garden struggled against the oppressive heat.

"Hello," he called.

John ducked out of the low house and squinted into the light. "Kody, my friend. Long time no see."

Kody dropped to the ground and crossed to grasp John's forearm as they squeezed each other's arms in greeting. John wore a faded red shirt and gray trousers, his hair braided much the same as Kody's.

"My friend," said Kody, "I have missed you."

"And I you."

And then Morning stepped from the house. She had dusky, flawless skin and wore a sandy-brown dress that would have been shapeless on another woman, but tied at her waist, it emphasized this woman's willowy frame.

She rushed to Kody's side. "It is good to see you."

Kody's gaze slipped past the pair to the open doorway. "Where is she?"

Morning turned and called softly. "Star, come and greet a friend."

A dark-haired child appeared in the doorway.

Kody stared. "She's grown."

"She's four years old now." Morning's voice held a touch of humor.

"She's beautiful." Kody couldn't take his eyes off her.

Morning held out her hand and the child hobbled toward her.

Kody's response was so sudden, so intense, it took his breath away. His gut twisted like he'd eaten something tainted. He took a step toward the child. John's hand on his arm stopped him. He forced air into wooden lungs.

"Her foot." He managed to grate the words past clenched teeth. He hadn't seen her since she was a baby. Had never seen her try to walk.

"It has always been crooked," John explained in low tones so the child wouldn't hear. "We hoped it would get better when she started to walk. You can see it hasn't."

Kody had noticed when she was tiny that her foot curled but he figured it was normal and as she grew it would straighten.

Star reached Morning and took her hand. "Momma?"

Her sweet, innocent voice grabbed Kody by the throat. He should have thought about this more. But he would never have guessed how it affected him to see Star again.

"Star, this is our good friend, Kody Douglas. Say hello."

"Hello, Mr. Kody Douglas."

Kody knelt on rubbery knees, his heart ready to burst from his chest with emotions so totally unfamiliar and unexpected he had no idea how to contain them or tame them.

"Hello, Miss Star. I'm pleased to see you." He touched her shoulder, let his hand linger for a moment, but as the ache inside him grew, he pulled his hand back and put two more inches between them. Immediately he changed his mind and leaned closer. This child had dark eyes, laced through and through with golden highlights. Unusual in an Indian. He supposed others noticed it, too.

"We knew you would return." John's voice pulled him back to reality.

He pushed to his feet. "I didn't intend to." He remembered Charlotte. She stood at the mare's side, watching with narrowed eyes.

A tremor snaked across his skin. She couldn't

have guessed the truth. "This is Miss Charlotte Porter. I'm taking her to my folks."

The Eaglefeathers welcomed Charlotte. John brought two chairs from the house and insisted they sit while he added bits of wood to the fire. Morning hustled about preparing something to eat. Charlotte followed Morning, begging to be allowed to help, until Morning gave her the job of frying bannock.

Star settled on the ground nearby, playing with a corncob doll.

"How are your folks?" John asked.

"Haven't heard from them since I left."

John and Morning exchanged looks.

"Have not seen them in some time." John chased away a fly.

"Don't they still come out here for Bible lessons?" His attention clung to the child, happily playing.

"Leland got sick. He could not come."

Kody pulled his gaze to John. "Sick?" He couldn't remember Pa ever being sick.

John shrugged. "Probably fine now."

Morning and Charlotte passed around the simple food. The stew had no meat. Kody wondered what happened to the government's promise to provide beef. He took a closer look around, noted how thin the material in John's shirt was, the color faded to pink in many spots. Morning's dress seemed to be crafted from material not meant for a garment. Even Star's little dress showed signs of being rather worn.

Purple shadows filled the hollows. A golden sun hovered at the horizon.

"Another beautiful day gone." John's low voice filled with pleasure. "Another day of God's goodness. And now we have the pleasure of Kody and Miss Charlotte's company."

Kody nodded, glad the drought and depression hadn't affected his friend's faith. Neither John nor Morning would presume to question Charlotte about how she and Kody met. And Charlotte didn't seem about to explain. That left Kody and he sketched the details.

"God has a plan for you," Morning said when he finished.

Charlotte looked startled.

Morning turned to Kody. "And you, too, my friend. He has brought you together for His purpose."

Kody and Charlotte looked at each other. They met by accident, each of them compelled to change their plans because of the other. He figured neither saw it as a blessing. Charlotte flashed a quick smile filled with triumph, then ducked her head. Kody understood Morning's simple faith echoed her own.

He would not express his doubts to Morning. The good woman had been so hospitable. It would be downright rude to argue with her.

The sun flashed its last light in dying pinks, and then the sky turned the color of water where the fishing was best, then indigo. In a few minutes the only light came from the fire, closing them in. The best time for sharing secrets, admitting intimate details that remained hidden in the light of day.

Only, Kody didn't intend to let any secrets pour forth.

At least not until Charlotte slept soundly out of earshot.

Morning rose gracefully. "Come, Miss Charlotte. I will show you where you can sleep." She scooped up the drowsy Star and carried her inside.

Kody and John sat in companionable silence, listening to the rustle of the women and child preparing for bed. Kody waited until they grew quiet. He waited some longer, but knowing Charlotte must be exhausted after riding all day, he figured she'd fall asleep as soon as her bones settled.

He turned to John and spoke softly yet urgently. "How is she? Really. Do the others accept her?"

"Everyone knows she isn't our child. And her eyes are light. They wonder who she is. They ask questions. But no one says anything bad."

"No one has guessed she's my child?"

"No one has said that's what they think. I see them whispering behind their hands, though."

"They must never know."

John sat in silence for some time. Kody knew he had more to say on the subject. He could keep talking, trying to keep John from speaking his piece. It would be futile in the end. John would sit quietly, nonjudgmental, until Kody grew silent, then say what was on his mind. So Kody waited. Might as well get it over with.

"What do you have to hide?" John's soft voice gave away nothing, but Kody knew his friend did not approve of his choice, although he would never come right out and say so.

"I don't fit in the white world or the Indian one. I don't want that for Star. I want her raised to belong here."

"We love her as our own."

That went without saying, so Kody didn't bother responding. Instead, he asked, "What about her foot? Has a doctor looked at it?"

John poked at the fire for a few minutes, sending sparks into the air. Finally he sat back. "I try once to take her to doctor in Favor. Big fat nurse chase me away. 'No Indians allowed,' she say. Government send doctor to reservation. I take Star to him. He look at foot and say only we can do nothing. 'Be satisfied she happy.'"

Kody gave a long sigh. She'd already borne the brunt of prejudice, then. Weariness filled his bones. He knew he couldn't expect anything more. Not many people were like Ma and Pa, who didn't care about Kody's heritage.

"So there's absolutely nothing you can do?"

"One thing. Doctor say there are special shoes. They cost much money."

Kody nodded. "I will get her those shoes."

"And then you will be gone again?"

"It is for the best."

John grunted. "For you?"

The question skidded along Kody's nerves. It was for Star, of course. She was better off without him. "She can't belong to two worlds. It doesn't work. Take it from someone who knows."

John grunted again but didn't speak. Just when Kody decided he didn't intend to, John murmured, "You are man with much war inside your head."

It was Kody's turn to grunt. John might have a point but this was not about his own needs. He had to do what he thought best for Star.

Chapter Six

The next morning, Charlotte thanked Morning and John for their hospitality. They were a kind couple, generous Christians willing to share what little they had. And Star was a sweet child, loved and cherished by them. She'd brought her corn-husk doll to Charlotte and told her about her doll being lost and found again. Charlotte didn't know if the story was imaginary or real, but she heard the underlying themes of loss and uncertainty. Perhaps common enough in a child, but poignantly more real in this little girl.

It was about more than she could do to keep from shooting an accusing look at Kody.

She restrained her confrontation until they rode away from the Eaglefeather home, until they both turned and waved for the last time. Then, as they rounded a bend blocking them from sight, she turned on him. "I overheard your conversation last night."

Shock widened his eyes, revealed itself on his face.

She didn't give him a chance to offer useless explanations. "I can't believe you would deny your own daughter."

His face turned into an expressionless mask. "I want your promise to never reveal this secret."

She shook her head. "How can you treat her like this? Is it because she's crippled? I heard John say nothing could be done. Are you ashamed of her?"

He allowed Sam to pick up the pace so he rode several feet in front of her, making further conversation impossible.

But Charlotte's anger had been building throughout the night and this morning as they drank tea and ate breakfast. She kicked the black mare. "Come on, Blackie, hurry up."

Kody snorted and glanced over his shoulder. "Since when did the old thing have a name?"

"Since right now. Even an animal deserves recognition." She managed to narrow the distance between them. "Do you have any idea how that child will feel when she finds out her father abandoned her? And where is her mother?"

"Her mother died shortly after her birth."

"I'm sorry." So Kody was Star's only parent. He needed to give that some importance in his plans. "It's simply not fair to ride off and leave someone behind like you're doing."

He reined in Sam and faced her. "I can never figure out if you mean yourself when you say such things."

"Me? This isn't about me. It's about Star. And you."

"Is it? Are you sure? Aren't you the least bit angry with Harry for leaving you behind?"

"Of course I'm upset." Harry had promised Charlotte would always have a home with him—a promise he seemed to forget on occasion. "I've done my best to always be pleasing and obedient." She swallowed back the torrent of words rushing from her memories of how she'd bent over backward trying to help and please. It hadn't seemed to make a difference in the long run. She shifted her thoughts to the most promising one—Mother's admonitions to be quick to obey, eager to help, easy to get along with. "That way," Mother said, "Harry will always be glad to provide you a home." When she rejoined Harry, Charlotte vowed he would never have cause to dismiss her.

Kody lifted his eyebrows and waited as if expecting more explanation, which, she decided, he wouldn't be getting.

"You don't have to walk away. You can try and change things. I envy you your choices."

"What's stopping you from making choices? You're white and free."

"You're male and free. That gives you choices I'm not allowed. Harry and his family are my only relatives."

He snorted. "Why don't you grow up and admit you're old enough to move on? Forget Harry. It seems he hasn't any trouble forgetting you."

Anger, so gut level and undeniable, roared through her like a duster with no barrier to break the wind. It sucked at her defenses, left her weak with fear and uncertainty. "He's not forgotten. I'll be joining him soon." She said it out of habit and desperation, unable to contemplate an alternative. But Kody's words forced her to face the unwelcome truth. Harry had left her behind. He'd easily abandoned her. Where had she failed? Was God really protecting her? Working out things for her good? Questions with no answers, and she didn't care one bit for Kody constantly poking at this sore spot.

She sucked in hot, dusty air. She wouldn't let Kody make this about her. "Sooner or later Star will realize Morning and John aren't her parents. John said himself people know she isn't their daughter. After all, a baby doesn't appear without some warning. And she had those light eyes. Was her mother white?"

"Half-breed like me."

"Can you imagine the questions and doubts Star will have when she figures out the truth? Where is my father? Why doesn't he care about me? What did I do wrong? As if a baby could be responsible for what an adult does. Poor little girl." She'd never expressed such vehement feelings before. Good little Charlotte. Always subservient. Always obedient and quiet, exactly like her mother said. Where did all this rage come from? She hardly recognized herself as she rushed on, unable to stem the frenzy of anger-driven words. "Doesn't she have enough to deal with—her mixed heritage, her crippled foot—without dealing with abandonment?" Her fury spent, she grew silent.

Kody pulled Sam to a halt, blocking Blackie's progress.

"She is better off on a reservation than with me. She will be accepted as an Indian. She would never be accepted as a half-breed in a white world. I forbid you to mention again that I am her father."

She sniffed disdainfully.

He continued to block her escape. "Your word."

She struggled with the instinct to comply. Good Charlotte always agreed. Readily. Quickly. Without argument. But good Charlotte seemed to have gone into hiding. "I will agree to no such thing."

He reached for the bridle, but she saw his intent to hold her there until she gave in and jerked Blackie to one side, laughing at the surprise on Kody's face.

He lunged after her, but slow-moving Blackie astonished them both by sidestepping out of his reach.

He moved Sam after her. "I will not allow you to cause my daughter—" He stopped. "I will not allow you to cause Star problems. Like you say, she has enough already."

"As you kindly pointed out, I know what it's like to be abandoned. This isn't the first time I've experienced it. And I have to say it doesn't get easier even when you get older. If there is anything I can say to make you care about Star…"

"I care about her," he shouted. "Can't you see that? Leaving her is the hardest thing I've ever done, but it's for her good."

She turned and faced him. "Then I guess someone needs to prove to you it isn't the best thing for her."

He laughed mirthlessly. "Ought to be quite a challenge." He looked at her steadily as if measuring and assessing, then he flicked the reins and Sam trotted down the road leaving Blackie and Charlotte to suck in his dust.

Charlotte settled into her slower pace. She'd tried. She could only pray Kody would think about her words. That someone would convince him he was wrong.

Too bad he planned to head to Canada as soon as he was rid of her. If they had some time together, she might be the one to do it.

She watched him, relaxed in the saddle, his braids swinging across his shoulders. Even from the back she read his defiance. She figured he challenged the world. No doubt he'd faced prejudice. But running hardly seemed the answer, especially when he had a sweet little daughter to keep him here.

Thinking of him leaving pinched her stomach as if a pin had come open and jabbed in her gut. He was the only person she knew. Everything else familiar and safe had been taken from her.

She laughed softly. Only two days ago she hadn't felt the least bit safe with him. Now she did. She'd miss Kody when he left, and acknowledging it gave her a vacant sensation—a different sort of feeling than the one of the past week as she struggled with missing Harry.

But how she felt didn't matter. She had until they reached Favor to convince him to be a father to little Star.

She nudged Blackie to go faster so she rode at

Kody's side. He glanced at her as she jogged up to him. His eyes narrowed with annoyance and probably a liberal dose of anger. She could hardly expect to win him over if he was mad. So she smiled and said nothing. She'd wait. For now. Just not long. Every step brought them closer to Favor, where he would deliver her to his parents and turn back north.

After a few minutes, he sighed, and relaxed into his saddle.

Did he think she'd forgotten the whole thing? Strangely enough, not many days ago she would have, rather than risk offending someone. But she had nothing to lose in this situation. And Star did. *Lord, guide me. Give me words that will change his mind.*

Suddenly he grabbed her horse and turned from the trail.

"What do you think—"

"Shh." The urgency in his voice filled her with alarm, and she kicked Blackie to follow Sam into the cluster of trees.

"Get down," he whispered, catching her before her feet hit the ground and rushing her behind some rocks.

He pulled off his hat and slowly peered out. Then he motioned her to keep low and look. She edged over until she glimpsed around the rocks.

They were a few yards from joining the main road, and two men slouching on horses headed toward Favor.

She dropped out of sight and sank to the ground. "Ratface and Shorty," she whispered.

"You named them?" He shook his head, no doubt recalling her words that even animals deserved recognition.

She rolled her eyes to indicate it didn't mean the same thing.

He hunkered down beside her. She wasn't fooled by his relaxed posture. She sensed his alert readiness. She glanced to where he'd hastily tied the horses and wished she'd thought to grab Harry's rifle. But she dared not move now and give away their hiding place.

Ratface and Shorty drew closer. She made out their words.

"We're gonna find that Injun and his white squaw, and when we do, we're gonna make them pay."

"Something about that woman don't sit right. Where'd she come from?"

"She was hiding. Probably didn't want anyone to see her with a savage."

Charlotte held her breath and prayed as never before. If the pair turned this direction, heading for the reservation, they would surely see Kody and her. And if they somehow didn't, then John, Morning and Star would be at risk.

Obviously thinking the same thing, Kody leaned forward, preparing to spring into action.

"Let's see what we find in this here town first."

"Something to drink maybe."

"Maybe."

Charlotte's breath eased out as the men continued on the main road.

Their conversation faded, but neither Kody nor Charlotte moved.

Finally Kody rose and edged up so he could see past the rock. "They're gone, but I guess we'll wait here awhile."

"Suits me just fine." She sucked in a few steadying breaths, then chuckled.

"What's so funny?"

"Shorty's still wondering where I came from. Scared him good."

"You hear the rest of what they said?"

She knew what he meant, figured he wanted to hear how she felt about it. "About me being a squaw?" She shrugged. "Silly, scared, evil men. Of course they think evil of others. Did you see the horses they're riding? And the guns? Where do you suppose they got them?"

"Probably stole 'em."

"What if they killed someone?"

"Not much we can do about it."

She sighed. There were far too many things a person couldn't do anything about.

Kody sank to the ground beside her.

There was one thing that could be changed. One thing she might be able to do something about. She prayed again for wisdom to use her words wisely, then began talking as if interested only in passing time. "I was ten when my mother died. Harry is eleven years older than me and as my only living relative, became my guardian. Mother knew she was dying and did her best to prepare me."

Kody shifted so he looked into her face. "Hard to prepare a child for such a thing."

Charlotte smiled. "Mother did a good job. I knew Harry was stuck with me, and it was up to me to make sure he didn't regret it."

"By being compliant?"

For some reason she disliked that word, probably because he said it with such contempt. "By helping and being agreeable."

He nodded. "Compliant. Submissive."

She'd always thought those characteristics highly desirable, but he made them sound less than ashes from yesterday's fire. She wanted to argue. Totally not a Charlotte reaction. She dismissed the desire and continued with her story, intent on her reason for telling of her hurtful past. "Harry married Nellie when I was barely twelve. I tried so hard to please her. But instead, I only seemed to succeed in making her angry." She drew in a deep breath. It still hurt to think of that troubled time. "Finally she insisted Harry find me a position somewhere else. He sent me to work for the Applebys." She tried to keep the bitterness from her voice, tried to stop the memories from hurting. She closed her eyes for a moment. *God, help me say what I want to say without having to live those feelings again.*

She opened her eyes, saw Kody watching her carefully and lowered her gaze. Had he seemed sympathetic, understanding? That might serve her well. She looked at him again. His dark eyes were steady, filled with bottomless concern. Something jolted through her in a rush, like a hot wind blowing away debris, sweeping clean the land. She wanted him to understand, to care about what happened to her. Unable to break from this unexpected sensation, she picked up her story. "The Applebys didn't consider me a part of their family. I served them, then ate my meals alone in the kitchen. I wasn't allowed to visit with either of the girls, who were around my age." She stopped, unable to say anything more, unwilling to share her shame at the rest of what happened. "It was the hardest time of my life. I'd lost my mother and now I might as well have lost my brother. I loved him and needed to be with him. I needed to know someone cared about me."

Kody grunted. "Seems rather cruel to send you away."

She leaned forward, eager to make him see how his case bore similarities. "He had his reasons, just like you think you do. He had a new wife who resented me in her home. I suppose I annoyed her. I know I argued with her a time or two." She'd quickly learned to avoid doing so, though it seemed very little she did pleased Nellie.

"Still, he is your brother and guardian."

She sat back. "And you are Star's father. How is it any different?"

He sighed. "It is. In so many ways. You're just too wrapped up in your own experiences to be willing to admit it."

Charlotte jutted out her jaw. "I suppose you expect her to understand all your very noble reasons?"

"She'll never need to know them because—" he grabbed her hand, resolve blazing from his eyes "—because she will never know she has a father other than John."

Charlotte pulled her gaze from his demanding stare. She rolled her head back and forth. "She will know someday. It's inevitable. As is the pain of rejection she will feel." She faced him squarely, boldly, determination making her voice hard. "You are the only one who can prevent that." She extricated her fingers from his grasp.

"You know nothing about what she'll have to deal with." He stalked over to the horses, led Blackie to her, helped her up, then jumped on Sam's back and kicked him into a trot.

Charlotte followed at Blackie's slower pace. She'd failed to convince Kody to change his mind. How long before Star realized she wasn't Morning and John's daughter? Before someone pointed out the impossibility and began speculating who her parents really were?

The poor child deserved to be spared the pain of such uncertainty and rejection.

As Blackie plodded along, Charlotte prayed for a miracle. She saw a town in the distance. Favor. *Lord, I've about run out of time*.

Kody reined Sam about and trotted to her side. "We're almost there. You have to promise not to say anything about Star to my ma and pa."

Shock like a cold drenching shivered down her skin. "They don't know they have a granddaughter?"

"No one knows about Star but Morning and John. And my secret is safe with them."

Charlotte stared at him. She realized her mouth hung open and she stiffly closed it. "You can't—"

"No. You can't. You can't say anything. Give me your word."

She narrowed her eyes and met his hard look. Compliant, he'd called her, making it sound like something small and annoying. Well, he was about to find out she could be *non*-compliant. "I will make no such promise." The heat of her words surprised her. She didn't know she had it in her to argue so vehemently.

"Then I won't take you to my parents." He waited, expecting her to give in.

"I never asked you to in the first place." She jerked Blackie away and rode onward.

Muttering, he caught up and rode at her side. "What do you plan to do?"

She had no plan, but she wasn't about to confess it to him. "First, I'll check and see if a letter has arrived from Harry." One couldn't have arrived yet, but she said it airily as if her heart didn't quake with fear of being on her own. As if she didn't shudder at the thought of seeing Ratface and Shorty.

She pushed away her scaredy-cat thoughts. She knew how to work. She'd find someone and throw herself at their mercy. Likely that was what he thought she should do. "You're right. I've been far too compliant and submissive. It's time I stepped out of my safe little world." She sucked in hot, dry air. "I'm sure I can find a position somewhere—chambermaid at a hotel, waitress, nanny…" It sounded easy, but she couldn't imagine walking up to a stranger and asking for work.

He snorted. "I can just see it. You'll jump at the first opportunity someone hands you, even if it's a wolf in sheep's clothes."

She stared straight ahead. Not even in exchange for a promise of rain would she let him see her fear of finding her way in an unfamiliar world. It was his fault she was in this situation. "If you'd just left me waiting for Harry… But no. You had to badger me until I agreed to leave with you, promising I'd be safe with your parents." She might have left out a few details like being out of water, like having Lother expect she'd marry him, like having the sheriff offer her a ride back to Big Rock. She shuddered. The sheriff actually thought she'd be glad to go with him straight into Lother's arms.

Kody rode at her side. "I really don't have a choice." He sounded as exasperated as she felt. "I'll take you to my parents as I promised. What you do after is up to you. But only on one condition—you promise not to tell them about Star."

The horses stopped moving as Kody and Charlotte stared at each other, measuring, challenging, considering.

Charlotte did not want to agree. She understood too well the pain the child would feel when she learned the truth or guessed parts of it. But she couldn't face riding into a strange town on her own. Her inner turmoil raged for several minutes. Then she nodded. "I'll leave it to you to tell them."

"Fine."

She noticed the irrigation ditches and the green fields fed by the life-giving water. If Harry had settled here, life would have been very different for them. Of course, Harry did not have money to buy land in such a prosperous area.

An hour later, they rose into the outskirts of Favor. She leaned forward. A pulse of life and activity radiated from the town. It had been so long since she'd felt the sense of hope the busy town expressed. She smoothed her hair and gave her dress a good study—wrinkled and dirty from wearing it for days and covered with evidence of the dusty trail. Suddenly she wasn't anxious to be seen by others. Not in this condition.

She ducked her head and wished she had a wide-brimmed hat to pull down to hide her face.

Kody sat up straight, facing ahead. "No point in trying to hide. People will look twice to see who is accompanying the savage."

"This has nothing to do with you. I don't want people to see me so dusty and untidy. Besides, how do you know they think that? Seems being the preacher's son would prove otherwise."

"You might think so."

He looked as if a stick had been shoved the length of his spine, so rigid was his posture.

They passed a big house with a tended yard and picket fence. An older man worked on the flower beds. He glanced up at the sound of their passing. Slowly he straightened, pushed his hat back and stared.

"Don't think he's thinking *preacher's son*. Nope. He's thinking *savage*. No doubt wondering if you've been captured."

"Well, I've not." She smiled and waved at the man. "Your flowers are pretty," she called.

The man beamed. "Thank you." He squinted in Kody's direction. "Aren't you Kody Douglas?"

Kody muttered to Charlotte, "You couldn't just ride on? No. You had to call attention to me being here." He touched the brim of his hat. "Hello, Mr. Blake."

Mr. Blake stared after them as Kody urged Sam forward.

"Seems like a nice man," Charlotte said.

"Huh."

"Has he treated you unfairly in the past?" She couldn't explain why she wanted to goad him. Unless to pay him back for how he pushed at her about sitting in the house waiting for Harry. Seemed like a good enough reason. "Is that the school?" She studied a two-story brick building with wide stairs leading to the double front doors. "I went to a school like that back in Kansas. Did you attend there?"

"A few years."

"You didn't finish?"

"Nope."

"This have anything to do with being part Indian?"

"Might have."

"I might as well squeeze the sky for water as try talking to you."

"Yup."

"What are you running from?"

"Who's running? Couldn't go much slower and still call it moving, now could we?"

She sniffed, annoyed beyond patience that he thought he could drag information from her and make a judgment on it, yet remain tight-lipped when it came to sharing anything about himself. "Some are accused of sitting around waiting for life to happen to them. Others seem to think it's superior to run from life."

They sauntered down Main Street past stately brick buildings. Cars and trucks lined the side of the street. A couple of wagons stood in front of a store. She read the sign: Benson's Feed and Mercantile. People hurried along the sidewalk. Another horseback rider pulled his mount to the hitching post in front of the post office. Despite her haughty words to Kody, she knew there would be no letter from Harry yet.

"Isn't that our friends, Ratface and Shorty?" He directed her gaze toward a pair skulking around the back of the bank. "Think they're planning to rob the place?"

Charlotte snorted. "Don't think they have the brains for anything that sophisticated."

The pair disappeared from sight and Charlotte relaxed again.

"This way." He turned down a side street.

She followed. She'd told him so much about herself. She wished she'd learned more about him, but it was too late to prod any more information from him.

She was about to meet her future.

Chapter Seven

Kody took in all the details of the town he hadn't seen in five years. A new store on Main Street. More houses past where the town used to end. More automobiles. Fewer horses.

Probably the same attitudes and prejudices.

He tightened his grip on the reins, forced himself to remain outwardly calm, giving no sign of emotion. Within minutes everyone in town would know he had returned. He steeled himself not to turn and ride away.

Then there it stood. The home where he'd been loved and welcomed. Emotions—long denied— choked him, clouding his vision. He blinked and stared, noted a bare patch on the roof where the shingles needed repairing. Then he widened his eyes and gave the place a hard look. It could do with a paint job. And an overhanging tree branch threatened the back porch. Strange Pa hadn't trimmed it. He'd always been mighty particular about such things. John said Pa had been sick. Kody narrowed his eyes. A ready, waiting tension tightened his muscles. What if Pa had died? Or Ma? He had to find out. He jumped from Sam and reached over to help Charlotte off the mare.

She smoothed her dress and hair. "I'm afraid I don't look my best. I feel like I'm wearing a coat of dust."

"Won't matter to Ma." Ma never judged a person by their clothes or their situation.

Or the color of their skin.

Not everyone proved so charitable. Ma and Pa had been hurt many times because of comments about Kody. Many people didn't understand how they could give a half-breed a home, a name and their love.

He hesitated at the gate. Why bring that pain back into their lives? He could simply leave Charlotte with instructions to find her way into the house and introduce herself. Ma would welcome her without question. He could jump back on Sam and…

But he wasn't strong enough to deny himself a chance to see his parents. To assure himself they were both okay. To receive again their love and acceptance. He despised his weakness.

The gate squealed a protest and dragged on the ground as he pushed it open. The top hinge needed fixing. His muscles twitched. Something was very, very wrong with the whole picture.

He waved for Charlotte to follow him and quietly crossed the yard, every nerve at attention, taking in every shadow, every corner. The only sound as they reached the door came from the birds in the trees. His boots echoed on the wooden steps. He paused. Did he knock or burst through the door as he had as a child? Not knowing what awaited him on the other side, he decided to knock.

The door opened slowly. "Yes?"

"Ma." He stepped into full view. "Ma." He hoped his voice didn't sound as rough as it felt.

"Kody, my son." Her arms went around him in the way he remembered, her hair tickling his cheek, her hands patting his back.

He hugged her tight, let himself be her boy again for just a few seconds, then pushed away to study her face. Lines had deepened around her eyes, creasing her cheeks. She seemed thinner. Her hair had turned gray before he left home— probably because of the worry he caused her. "Ma, how are you?"

"Dakota Douglas, it's been almost five years." Her voice tightened and tears wet her cheeks.

Kody didn't know if he should retreat or wait for the dressing-down he knew he deserved. He chose the latter.

"Five years, Kody, without a word. I didn't know if you were even alive. Where have you been?" She shook him gently. "Never mind. You're here now. An answer to my prayers." She hugged him again. "It's so good to have you back."

"Ma, I'm not staying."

"Why not? This is your home."

"It's better if I leave."

Her eyes clouded with what he supposed was sadness. "I guess you have to do what you think best." She tugged at his arm. "Come in." Then she saw Charlotte. "You've brought company?"

"Ma, this is Charlotte Porter. She needs someplace to stay until she can join her brother."

Ma took Charlotte's hand and pulled her inside. "Any friend of Kody's is more than welcome."

Charlotte's expression grew cautious. "We aren't really friends. He just found me and said—"

"Well, you're welcome, anyway." Ma's look at Kody suggested he'd somehow been amiss. He couldn't imagine how. He'd brought Charlotte here despite his reservations—the word again brought a smile to his lips.

Ma drew them into the kitchen. "Sit down and tell me everything," she said to Kody. "Wait, I'll make tea. Everything is better over a cup of tea." As she bustled around filling the kettle and pulling out teacups, Charlotte went to her side.

"How can I help, Mrs. Douglas?" She hesitated then in a softer voice, added, "If you're to provide me shelter, then I intend to repay it by helping as much as I can."

Ma gave Charlotte a gentle smile. "I appreciate your offer, but we'll settle that later. I'm sure there will be lots of ways you can prove yourself useful."

Kody stood in the middle of the room, his insides so tight it would have been impossible to bend enough to sit. "Where's Pa?" He couldn't imagine how he'd deal with an announcement that something had happened to the man who taught him most everything he knew.

"Resting. He had a hard night."

Kody's breath went out in a noisy rush. He sat down quickly to hide the relief leaving him weak in the knees. Pa sometimes sat with the sick and dying and troubled. But he didn't nap long even when he'd missed a night or more of sleep. He'd be striding through the door any minute, calling to Ma to put the kettle on. Kody filled his lungs with heart-calming air for the first time since he'd noticed the disrepair of the house. Pa had been busy, was all.

Ma poured tea and sat down. "How did you meet Charlotte?"

Kody filled in the details with some help from Charlotte. Ma laughed as Charlotte described her anger at her brother for leaving her a gun with no ammunition.

"Sounds to me like you've got lots of spunk," Ma said.

Kody grinned widely. "You don't know the half of it." As he told of Charlotte chasing off the two robbers with the same empty gun, his heart swelled with admiration.

"I trust God to take care of me and He does," she said with perfect calm and assurance.

Good thing she trusted God because it seemed she couldn't trust her brother. He wondered, not for the first time, what sort of man Harry was. To think of Charlotte there alone, Lother only a mile away. If the man had realized…

Ma squeezed Charlotte's hand. "I can truthfully say the same for myself. He has never failed me." Ma turned to Kody. "I pray you continue to believe it, too."

Kody shifted his gaze toward the front-room door, hoping to see his father, but he felt Ma's expectant waiting. Finally her silence forced him to look back. "Ma, I know what you believe is true. But I'm not sure it's for me."

He wished he could pull the words back as Ma's expression registered shock, sadness and pain.

"Oh, Kody. You once believed. I know you did. What happened? Where have I failed?"

"Ma, you didn't fail, but my life just doesn't fit into neat little packages like yours and Pa's do."

"Are you suggesting we believe because we haven't faced difficulties?"

"Of course not. No one has a life without troubles. But you know who you are." He wished she'd let it go. He didn't want to hurt her. Nor did he want Charlotte to witness this.

"You know who you are, too. You are Dakota Douglas. My son. You are loved and special."

He sighed. "I've never doubted your love. But there are things outside of that. Let's not discuss it anymore." He had avoided Charlotte's eyes, but now sent her what he hoped passed as an apologetic look. When he saw the challenge in her eyes, he doubly wished he'd sidestepped the conversation. He suspected she'd somehow take this whole scenario and twist it to mean something more than it did. Somehow she'd make it about Star. "Where's Pa? Shouldn't he be up by now?"

Ma pushed her chair back and sighed. "I guess it's time for you to see him."

Kody did not like the way Ma's voice seemed so tired. Something simply wasn't right.

"Come along."

Charlotte remained seated.

"You, too," Ma insisted. She led them past the living room into his parents' bedroom.

Pa lay in bed, staring at the ceiling, covered by a patchwork quilt Kody remembered, made of fabric Ma had salvaged from worn-out trousers.

"Leland, Kody's home."

Pa didn't move. Didn't even blink. His skin had never been such a washed-out pasty color, nor his mouth so slack.

Kody stared. "What's wrong with him?"

Ma sat on the edge of the bed and took one of Pa's hands. "He's had a stroke. He's improving every day, though."

Kody did not want to know what he'd been like before the improvement.

"Come," Ma said. "Sit where he can see you."

Kody hesitated. This unresponsive, shrunken man was not his father. He was a stranger, a frightening shell of a man. Looking at him made Kody want to run upstairs to the bed where he'd slept as a child and hide his face in the pillow. Pretend things were exactly as he remembered them. That nothing had changed since he left. But he couldn't hide from the facts, so he crossed to the bed and sat where Ma indicated.

His father turned slowly and, with what seemed like great effort, pulled his gaze to Kody. He mumbled something that might have been "Hello."

Kody tried not to think of the man his father had been last time he saw him and smiled in spite of the tightness starting in his toes and spiraling upward to the corners of his mouth. "Hello, Pa. It's been a while."

Pa lifted one hand a few inches from the bed-covers and mumbled. Kody thought it sounded like his name. Suddenly his love for this man overcame his shock. He bent over and hugged his father, breathing in the smell of soap and moth-balls.

When he straightened, his father's cheeks were damp with tears.

Ma grabbed a hankie and dried them. "He's so glad to see you. As am I."

Pa struggled with wanting to say something. Finally he got out the words, "You stay?"

Kody wished he didn't understand his father's question, but he did. He wished he could give the answer his father wanted, but staying this close to Star made it impossibly hard to pretend his daughter didn't exist. If people learned she was his, their prejudice would undo the four years of sacrifice he'd already endured.

Yet how could he leave his parents under these circumstances? "I'll stay a few days, then I must be on my way." Long enough to fix the roof and prune the tree, if nothing else.

He waited until they were back in the kitchen before he bombarded Ma with questions. "When did this happen? How have you managed? Is he going to get better?"

Ma bustled about pulling potatoes from the bin in the pantry. "It's been a couple of months now. But he started to have weak spells before that." She seemed distracted by meal preparations, so Kody waited. He'd get his answers sooner or later.

Charlotte stood by offering to help.

Ma gave her a knife and a basin of potatoes. "I don't mind if you peel these." She opened the icebox and pulled out an already cooked roast. "I wondered how I'd use this all up when I cooked it yesterday. The Johnsons brought it. People have been so good to us. Even though your father hasn't been able to perform his preaching duties, many still make sure we have enough."

Kody wondered how true that was or if Ma maintained her positive attitude out of habit. As he recalled, even when Pa preached every Sunday, the offerings were skimpy. Most people gave in the way of food. He choked back his anger. Ma and Pa were good, kind people. They didn't deserve this misfortune.

Charlotte put the potatoes on to boil, then quietly went to Kody's side. "I'd like to bring in my belongings."

"I'll help you." He needed to get his mind on other things besides the unfairness of this situation.

When they reached the horses, Charlotte grabbed his arm and forced him to face her. Tears clung to her eyelashes. Her smile quivered. "What a blessing you returned. See how God works things out? He knew you were needed at home."

The approval in her voice gave him a warm feeling; the weight of her hand on his arm, the way she touched him without aversion, sent a sudden skitter of pleasure to his heart. But it didn't change the facts of life.

He looked at her hand on his arm and backed away, forcing her to drop her arm to her side.

He knew he'd embarrassed her, made her think he minded her touching him. It wasn't the case. If things were different, if he was a different person... But he wasn't. And he couldn't change the facts. He didn't belong in the white world, wasn't accepted on the reservation. And anyone associated with him would be marked for the same narrow-mindedness. How often had he heard people whisper cruel things about Ma and Pa? Some didn't even bother lowering their voices.

Charlotte took her things when he handed them to her, but set them on the ground. "I'll help with the horses."

He couldn't be bothered to argue, so she carried the bridles to the garage housing Pa's old car. At least Pa still had it so he could get out and around. Kody stopped so suddenly Charlotte jolted into his back.

"What's wrong?" she asked.

"Nothing." Perhaps Pa would never again need the car. Good thing he'd insisted Ma learn to drive, too. Kody took a deep breath. "Why does God allow such things? It just isn't fair."

Her eyes grew wide, but he didn't want to hear any more platitudes. He hurried to hang the saddles before she could come up with any sort of answer.

Chapter Eight

Charlotte followed Kody into the house. "I'm glad you're staying here for a bit."

He spun around so fast she stopped. She didn't much care for the way his eyes flashed, and she fell back a step.

"And why should you be glad?"

His voice had dropped to deeper tones, full of quiet warning, but she didn't let it stop her from speaking her thoughts.

"It will give you time to reconsider your decision to ride out of Star's life." God had provided her another chance to convince him. Perhaps this had been His plan all along, the reason she'd been left by Harry—in order to serve a purpose here. She'd known God had a plan, that He would turn things out for good.

And if it helped Star, well, it was quite fine with her.

"You promised you wouldn't say anything about her."

"To your parents. Not to you."

He grunted. "Don't expect me to be sitting around making small talk."

"Nope. But surely you wouldn't deny me the pleasure of your company once in a while." She felt telltale heat race up her cheeks, felt it burn deeper by the sudden awareness she wouldn't be averse to spending time in his company, and not for the sole purpose of discussing Star. Something about him proved both unsettling and steadying.

He quirked one eyebrow in mocking disbelief. His eyes narrowed as he took in the way her cheeks flared. Then he smiled, the gesture beginning at the corners of his mouth and working upward to his eyes.

At the way he looked at her, the heat in her cheeks spread to her chest, making her heart beat against her ribs in a most alarming way. Something alive, vibrant and vital, passed between them. She didn't know what to call it—interest, friendship or something exceeding both. She only knew the moment shifted her world, changed the way she looked at life, enticed her toward something new, exciting and deliciously frightening.

And then he grunted. "You are joking, of course." And he took the last two steps toward the door.

She didn't move, waiting for dizziness to pass. They'd shared a few special days and she embarrassingly admitted to a growing regard for him, yet he'd dismissed her feelings. Obviously he didn't return them. Yet how dare he toss her feelings aside as if they had no value? Anger stole past her usual complacent attitude. Why would he be any different from Harry and Nellie, or the Applebys, or Lother? Seems people treated her like a commodity. Use Charlotte or leave her. Whatever suits you.

She closed her eyes. *Lord forgive me. I belong to You, not people, no matter what they think. Help me be patient and cooperative.* Her anger fled as quickly as it came.

Only when peace settled back into her soul did she follow Kody indoors.

Mrs. Douglas wiped her hands on a worn towel. "The doctor said there's no reason he shouldn't do more. But he doesn't seem to have any interest in anything but lying in bed staring at the ceiling." She chuckled. "But I think having you here will make him want to get up. He won't want you to think he's laid down and quit."

"Is that what he's done?"

Mrs. Douglas sighed. "I've thought so a few times. I'm so glad God brought you back to us. It's bound to make a big difference. I think we should persuade him to join us for supper."

Charlotte understood they spoke of Kody's father. She hurried to the cupboard and took the towel from Mrs. Douglas. "Let me finish the supper preparations while you and Kody tend to your husband."

"Thank you, child."

Kody and his mother left the room, set on stirring Mr. Douglas from his comfortable bed. She smiled, thinking how persuasive Kody could be. Not with sweet talk, but with prodding and badgering. She tried to imagine him sweet-talking her, praising her, appreciating her. She grabbed the edge of the cupboard as an ache as wide as the South Dakota prairie tore through her. Then she pushed the idea from her mind. She wasn't so needy she hungered for approval from everyone she encountered. She drained the potatoes, mashed them to a creamy texture and spooned them high into the serving bowl, hoping Mrs. Douglas would appreciate her efforts.

She hummed as she worked. What a pleasure to be in a house with water as close as the turn of a tap, with a window overlooking a yard with trees, and filled with a spirit of joy and faith. She took the potatoes to the table. A piece of oilcloth in blue and yellow squares covered the wooden table. Crocheted pads, alternately blue and yellow, covered the seats of the six wooden chairs. Yellow medallions marched in straight lines up the pale-blue wallpaper. Several calendars hung in various places; one had pictures of mountains, another of an English landscape and two showed bright bouquets of flowers. Charlotte smiled, thinking if Nellie had hung such cheery pictures, instead of the stern likeness of her parents and a calendar boasting the latest threshing machine, they might all have benefited.

Charlotte set the bowl in the middle of the table between the platter of thinly sliced roast beef and the divided dish with four kinds of pickles and relish, and thanked God for the bounty.

The trio edged into the room, Mr. Douglas leaning heavily on Kody's arm. Charlotte hurried to hold a chair for the man. He wore a tan sweater buttoned over a dark blue shirt. His black trousers hung on his tall frame. His thinning white hair had been combed back by either Mrs. Douglas or Kody.

"Thank you, child," Mrs. Douglas said, breathing heavily as she bent over her husband. "That was a long walk for you. Are you okay?"

Mr. Douglas gave a crooked smile. "I'm fine." His speech was slurred yet discernible.

Mrs. Douglas sat down. "Let's pray."

Charlotte closed her eyes, as the woman folded her hands to say grace.

"Your gifts are so bountiful. My son is back home. My Leland walked to the table. We have a beautiful young woman to share with, and You have blessed us with plenty of food. My heart is full." Her voice thickened. "Too full for words," she whispered. "Amen."

Charlotte stole a glance at Kody. His eyes narrowed, his expression tightened as if forcing himself to mentally refute the words. He seemed determined to believe God's love and care did not extend to him. He blamed his race and people's prejudice, yet how could he deny this outpouring of love from God's heart through his parents and into his life?

Mrs. Douglas cut her husband's food into bite-size pieces, then wrapped his fingers around the fork handle and guided it toward the food.

He let his hand fall to the table and looked confused at the idea of feeding himself.

"You can do it, dear," Mrs. Douglas encouraged.

Her husband mumbled, sounding angry.

Charlotte caught her breath as he tried to capture a piece of meat. She let her lungs exhale when he succeeded in getting the meat into his mouth. His eyes glistened with angry defiance. Charlotte ducked her head to hide her amusement, knowing either anger or determination were healthy emotions to spur the man into fighting his way back from the ravages of his stroke.

Mrs. Douglas faced Kody. "Now tell me what you've done since you left home. I want to know everything."

Kody laughed. "Ma, we only have three hours until dark."

"Start with the condensed version and fill in the details later."

"Well, I worked in an irrigation ditch for a season. Didn't like mucking in the mud. Helped build some roads. The machinery's too noisy. I helped on a ranch for most of a year. I liked that work the best. But I needed to move on."

"Where? Where are you going, Kody? What are you looking for you can't find here where you belong?" Mrs. Douglas asked the questions, but Charlotte saw how Mr. Douglas focused on Kody, waiting for his answers.

"I'm heading for Canada."

"Why? What's in Canada?"

Kody's smile looked strained. "Space, Ma. They say there's places where a man can live and not see another human being for months."

Mrs. Douglas shook her head. "Sounds like a

lonely place to me. And I know you wouldn't be happy there. You've always been the sort to have lots of friends."

"Sometimes a man is better off alone."

Mrs. Douglas put her fork down and reached for Kody's hand. "We were sorry to hear Winnoa died. I know how that must have hurt. I figured that's why you disappeared. You needed time to get over that. We understood. But that's almost four years ago. Surely it's time to come home."

Kody shrugged. "I can never come home."

"Why?" Mrs. Douglas demanded, her voice thin with what Charlotte took for sorrow over her son's attitude. "What happened to make you change? We have always loved you and still do. You know that."

Charlotte watched the play of emotions in Kody's face—the desire to ease his mother's concern warring against his belief he belonged nowhere. She wanted to shout for him to notice how clearly he belonged here surrounded by his parents' love.

"Ma, this has nothing to do with you. You and Pa are the best parents anyone could wish for. This is about who I am. I said I'd stay a few days. I'll fix a few things and then I'm moving on."

Charlotte ducked her head because she knew Kody might be running from his life, but God had turned him around and brought him back—perhaps to give him a chance to see how much Star needed him, even for him to discover how much he loved the child. It satisfied her to think God might have chosen her to bring Kody back to his family. It almost made it worthwhile to have suffered fear, hunger and thirst, and to endure missing Harry and the family with such an ache.

A draft of loneliness blew through and left her empty and tired. She'd cared for five-year-old Ricky since his birth, reading him stories and playing little games to amuse him when Nellie was occupied. As he grew older she taught him how to tie his shoes, how to build a little farm out of sticks and marbles. And when Mandy came along eighteen months later, she'd done the same for the little girl.

Pain hit her with cruel force. Kody had what she wanted so badly it filled her mouth with a dry, dusty taste. He had love and a home.

She suddenly had difficulty breathing and kept her head down, struggling to control her emotions, grateful the Douglas family focused their attention on Kody.

"Charlotte?" Kody said.

Maybe they weren't as distracted as she hoped. She sucked in air, slowly filled her lungs, willed herself to cover her emotions with a smile and then she looked up.

"Are you all right?"

The concern in his face caused her smile to slip. Her eyes stung.

"Something's wrong."

She shook her head and lifted her hand to indicate she didn't want to talk about it. She dared not try to speak for fear of losing control.

Mrs. Douglas watched, her face full of concern, which further threatened Charlotte's self-restraint. She shifted, met Mr. Douglas's eyes and almost broke down at the compassion in them.

He nodded. "Sad," he said, as plain as if Kody had said the word. "Why?"

She might have ignored Kody's questions and sidestepped his mother's silent ones, but she couldn't ignore Mr. Douglas's.

"I miss my brother and his family," she managed to choke out. It wasn't the whole source of her sadness, only the beginning of it. Knowing Harry could walk away from her so easily reinforced an idea she'd been fighting since her mother's death. Harry didn't really want her, even though she'd done her best to follow Mother's instructions to be useful. No matter how hard she worked, how quickly she obeyed, how useful she tried to be, she was tolerated rather than welcomed.

Mrs. Douglas reached for her hand. "My dear,

forgive me. I've been so busy rejoicing over my own blessings, I've forgotten your troubles."

Charlotte managed a shaky smile. "It's okay. He's sending for me." He had to. She had no other home, no other family. She belonged with him, whether tolerated or welcomed.

Mrs. Douglas patted Charlotte's hand. "Well, you're more than welcome to stay here as long as you need. I'm mighty glad for the company."

There was the word she longed for—welcome. It hurt that it came from a stranger. How could Mrs. Douglas care about her when her only surviving family member so obviously didn't?

Mrs. Douglas leaned back and smiled at everyone around the table. "I think I owe it to you that Kody has returned. God works in mysterious ways."

"You and Charlotte both talk the same," Kody said. "As if bad things are a blessing in disguise."

Charlotte and Mrs. Douglas exchanged wide smiles. It had been a long time since Charlotte had known the pleasure of a shared faith with an older woman. Not since her mother's death. The idea of her being a stranger vanished. They were sisters in Christ.

Kody's mother voiced a thought for both of them. "Sometimes they are."

Mr. Douglas tried to speak. They waited as he

struggled with his words. "God's ways are always good. We have to believe that."

"Fine," Kody said. "God's ways might be good, but man's ways leave much to be desired."

Charlotte ached to point out God's love wasn't controlled by man's actions, but she struggled with sorting out the difference in her own mind and had no words of assurance to offer except those that expressed the faith she clung to. "God uses all things for our good."

"Amen," both Kody's parents said.

The pleasure of their shared faith was a balm to Charlotte's soul. She wished they would share ways they'd seen God turn things around, knew it would bolster her own struggling faith, but Mr. Douglas tried to push his chair back. "Bed."

Charlotte filled the basin with hot water and tackled the wall behind the stove. Mrs. Douglas had protested when Charlotte insisted she wanted to work, then confessed she could use help with the spring cleaning.

"I know it's long overdue, but somehow I haven't had the heart to do it."

Charlotte gladly took on the job. She loved to help, even without Mother's warning ringing in her ears. *There's nothing harder to tolerate than a homeless relative who contributes nothing.* Charlotte figured it applied equally to an uninvited guest.

As she worked, Charlotte listened to the sound of Kody repairing the roof.

He'd begun the job before breakfast as if he couldn't wait to get done so he could be on his way.

Somehow she had to devise some way to convince him otherwise and learn to deal with being Star's father. That required a chance to talk to him in private. And she knew he wasn't going to make it easy for her.

She didn't know how long she had. Perhaps today a letter from Harry had been forwarded to Favor.

But Mrs. Douglas returned from the post office without a letter for Charlotte. Charlotte smiled despite her disappointment. "Maybe tomorrow. In the meantime I have lots to keep me busy." And something she wanted to accomplish before she left.

By lunchtime, she'd washed the walls in the kitchen. Over the meal of thick, homemade tomato soup and hot biscuits, she said, "If I had a ladder I could wash the ceiling."

"I'll get something," Kody said, and after the meal, brought in a stepladder and set it in place. "Be careful."

She stared at his back as he retreated. He hadn't

worn his hat since he returned home, and the sun glistened on his hair as he stepped out the door.

His caution was only polite words with no particular significance, yet she couldn't stop herself from thinking he might care a little about her safety. As she stood on the ladder and scrubbed the smoke and flyspecks off the ceiling, she smiled, remembering how frightened she'd been of him just a few days ago. But he'd proved to be a gentleman, a loving son and a hardworking man.

She paused and looked at her work. She'd missed a spot and she leaned over, grabbing the top of the ladder as she stretched.

"Is this your idea of being careful?"

Kody's demanding voice startled her. She swayed, tried to steady herself but found only air to cling to. "No," she wailed as the ladder began to tip.

She closed her eyes, waiting for the crash, waiting to feel her body hit the hard floor. She gasped as, instead, she felt a warm, solid chest and strong arms holding her.

"Are you okay?" The breath of his soft words brushed her cheek.

She kept her eyes shut, too embarrassed to risk meeting his eyes. "I'm fine." She tried to step away but still off balance, succeeded in leaning into him more heavily. She grabbed for his chest.

His arms tightened around her. "Take it easy."

"I'm fine," she said again and managed to right herself and step back, then realized she held a scrap of paper. She must have caught it when she clutched his shirt for support. She glanced at it, then looked closer at the advertisement for special shoes for children with clubfeet. "Straighten your child's feet," it read.

He quietly took the paper from her fingers and returned it to his pocket. He didn't say anything, didn't move. He avoided her gaze as if embarrassed. She waited, not sure how to overcome the awkward moment.

Chapter Nine

Kody kept his hand over his pocket. John had given him the ad for the shoes. Kody intended to order a pair for Star before he left. In fact, he planned to do so this afternoon.

And get some supplies for the folks. He'd been to the basement to clean out the vegetable bins and noticed the shelves held only a few canning jars from last summer and one lone can of beans. Ma usually kept the shelves well stocked. Always said you never knew when you might have unexpected company or some emergency.

Charlotte waited as if expecting an explanation for the scrap of paper. No doubt she'd figured out what the shoes were for.

"Star needs a pair of special shoes."

"And you're going to get them?"

"Ain't like John can afford it."

"They appear to live a pretty meager life."

Her words seemed to slice through any defense. As if he was somehow to blame. But she didn't need to point out he had a responsibility to see Star had all she needed. Which meant seeing John and Morning had their needs met.

"I figured on getting a few things for them while I'm here."

"I'll help."

He finally relaxed at her eagerness. "How?"

"If I had some fabric I could make dresses for Morning and Star. And a shirt for John."

Her unexpected generosity made him look at her with fresh interest. She'd already impressed him with her gumption and her good humor. Again, he wondered how she really felt about Indians—and half-breeds. Was she only being charitable because they were poor unfortunates, or because she saw them as people like her with the same needs and wants and concerns? "The store has yard goods. If you go with me, I can buy what you need."

"Great. When do you want to go?"

"When will you be finished here?"

"Another hour?"

"I should finish the roof by then, too."

She nodded and began to turn away, then

stopped. "You care about your daughter more than you want to admit."

He gave her a warning look, silently reminding her of her promise, and glanced over his shoulder half expecting to see Ma standing in the front-room doorway. She wasn't, of course. He could trust Charlotte to be careful not to give away his secret.

An hour later, they headed toward the business section of town.

As they stepped inside the mercantile store, he noticed the way the room grew quiet. He expected as much. It had been the same since he was big enough to attract attention.

Charlotte didn't seem to notice, however. She rushed toward the yard goods and started to examine the bolts. "Look, this would be perfect for John." She held out a bolt of deep blue.

Ignoring the way Mr. Boulter watched his every move, Kody went to Charlotte's side. "He'd like that."

Within minutes, Charlotte picked out a fawn-colored material for Morning. She went through the stacks twice. "I don't see anything that's just right for Star." Charlotte signaled to the young woman hovering behind the counter and she hurried over. "Do you have anything else? I want something for a little girl."

"I do believe I have a couple more bolts in the back." She looked closely at Kody. "It's Kody Douglas, isn't it?"

Kody raised his eyes to the girl. "Amy Boulter?"

She nodded.

"You've grown up since I last saw you."

"I bet your parents are glad to see you."

"Amy—" Mr. Boulter spoke sternly "—is there something you should be doing?"

"Yes, Father." She leaned toward Charlotte. "I'll be right back." She flashed a smile at Kody. "It's good to see you." She scampered away and returned with two bolts of material. Charlotte oohed over the brown with little pink flowers. "That's perfect. Don't you think so?" She waited for Kody's approval.

Keenly aware several customers hung around watching the proceedings and no doubt drawing their own uncharitable conclusions, he readily agreed.

Amy cut off the requested lengths and carried them to the till.

Kody hung back and spoke low to Charlotte. "I want to get some things for Ma and Pa, too. Can you help?"

"Of course." She flashed him a smile. "I love shopping."

Together, with input from Amy, they decided what to buy. When Amy began to total the bill, her father edged her aside. "We can't give you credit. And I've given your parents all I can allow."

"Father!" Amy gasped.

"How much do they owe?" Kody demanded.

Mr. Boutler did some figuring. When he gave the total, Kody realized he wouldn't be able to order the shoes for Star until he earned more money. He pulled out his purse and practically emptied it.

Behind him, he heard a hoarse whisper. "Where do you suppose he got so much money?"

Mr. Boulter took the cash with undue haste as if expecting Kody to snatch it back. Only then did the storekeeper step aside to let Amy finish the order.

"I'm sorry," she said, her voice cracking. "Don't pay any attention. Not everyone is so close-minded." She sent a look at her father, clearly informing him who she considered to be exactly what.

Kody began to gather up the bundles.

Amy stopped him. "We'll deliver the order, won't we, Father?"

The man glowered at the three of them but didn't refuse.

Kody headed for escape, but Charlotte paused at the door.

"Thank you. It's been a pleasure doing business in your fine store."

He glanced over his shoulder to see she included Mr. Boulter in her smile. Then she nodded to the hovering customers.

"I'm sure I'm going to enjoy your beautiful town." Still smiling, she joined Kody.

He let his breath *whoosh* out as they headed for the post office. "Now you see the way it is."

"They have a good selection of most everything. I am really happy about the yard goods we chose."

Was she being purposely thick-headed? "You don't think I mean the things on the shelves, do you?"

She stopped and faced him with narrowed eyes. "What else would you mean?"

"I mean the way they acted, of course."

"Amy was very pleasant."

"Unlike her father."

"Some people are naturally more cheerful that others."

He stopped walking to stare at her. "You must have heard the people muttering behind us."

"Nothing wrong with my hearing as far as I know. But why let a few unjustified comments rob you of enjoying the fun we had or the welcome Amy extended?"

"That's a little nearsighted in my opinion."

She shrugged. "I learned a long time ago it was best to overlook insults. Otherwise I would be walking around all day nursing hurt feelings."

He jammed his hands into his trouser pockets and strode toward the post office. No point in trying to reason with someone who ignored anything that didn't fit into her belief that everything had a good and noble purpose. And perhaps it was best to let her cling to her idealized way of thinking. He didn't want her to deal with the harsher realities he faced.

He waited outside while she went in to check for a letter from Harry. When she cam out empty-handed he expected her to be disappointed, but she smiled.

"It gives me time to make those garments, time to see you get those little shoes for Star and—" she looked away and finished airily "—time to see you change your mind about being her father."

"I don't think you'll be around long enough. Because, lady, you will be long in your grave and still waiting."

"We'll see. In the meantime, I have some sewing to do."

"How come you argue with me all the time? Aren't you supposed to be cooperative?"

"Oh, yes. Good little Charlotte, meek and mild. Poke her hard and see her smile."

Her quiet tone did not deceive him. He'd touched a nerve. He didn't mean to hurt her, yet he enjoyed seeing her with a little spark.

"This something you heard before?"

"Only inside my head. Sometimes it's hard to be obedient and cooperative."

They turned off Main Street toward home. No longer did he feel as if eyes followed his every move. And he relaxed. "I like you better when you show some spunk, instead of sitting around waiting to be rescued." Then he began to laugh low and quiet so as not to attract attention from anyone who might be passing. "I'll never forget how you threatened me with a useless gun and sent those two scoundrels racing down the road with the same gun."

She grinned at him. "They deserved to be scared."

They stopped walking and faced each other. They didn't touch. Didn't make any gesture toward it. Yet the way she looked at him felt as real as if she'd brushed her hand over his cheek or squeezed his shoulder, friendly and reassuring with a hint of something unsettling, as if the imagined touch eased him toward the edge of a precipice.

He should step back from the force that seemed to bind him to her. He knew he ought to run as fast and far away from this woman as possible.

But he knew he wouldn't. Couldn't. Didn't want to. He had Star and his parents to think about, but only by dint of extreme concentration did they even enter his thoughts. It wasn't any of them holding him here on this spot, making him want to stay in Favor where he seemed unlikely to gain favor from anyone. Charlotte pretended to be all docile and cooperative. He guessed she'd been taught so by a mother who feared for her future. But he had seen glimpses of something fierce and strong in her. He wouldn't mind seeing what happened when that side finally escaped into the open. He figured it would, given time and some encouragement. He just might be the one to give her a little prod in that direction.

That evening, Pa agreed to sit in the front room after supper. Charlotte had a little dress almost sewn together. "You mother has a sewing machine. It makes things go quickly." She attached buttons as Ma read to Pa from the Bible. Kody wished he had something to do with his hands. Something to occupy his mind, to keep him from watching Charlotte and enable him to block the words from Ma's mouth. He relaxed significantly when Ma closed the Bible. Not that he didn't believe it. But he couldn't believe it included him.

Ma looked at Charlotte. "I expected you would be making a dress for yourself when you asked to use the sewing machine, but that's a child's dress."

Kody's lungs grabbed at his ribs and refused to operate. He didn't move, fearing his face would register his worry. But he gave Charlotte a look he wished could burn her face, make her glance at him and see his silent warning. But she kept her eyes on knotting a thread, then held up the little garment.

"We stopped at the reservation before we got here. I met some of Kody's friends."

Kody kept his eyes on her. *Be careful what you say.*

She flashed a quick smile as she continued, "They have so little. I offered to make a garment for each of them and Kody bought the goods."

Kody tilted his head a fraction. She'd done well. "They know the Eaglefeathers from teaching out there." He turned to Ma. "They befriended me when I went to the reservation."

"Good people. Sincere Christians. They always ask after you when we go. Of course we haven't been able to make it in some time. I was always glad to know you'd made some friends there."

He didn't bother saying how few he'd made. The Indians hadn't cared for a half-breed with white ways.

"When Kody left home, he went to the reservation," Ma explained to Charlotte. "I understood how he wanted to connect with that part or himself."

Kody watched Charlotte. Would she reveal any revulsion at being confronted with the facts? But she met Ma's eyes with open interest. "Kody says you adopted him?"

"He was ours from his first breath."

The way Ma said it always gave Kody a sense of well-being. But he wondered what Charlotte really thought of his mixed race. And what would she think if she knew his uncertain heritage? "Ma, tell her how you came to be stuck with me."

"Kody, what a dreadful thing to say. We weren't stuck. We were blessed." She turned to pat Pa's hand. "Weren't we, Leland?"

Pa waved a trembling hand at Kody. "Good boy."

The slurred words blessed Kody.

"You're right," Ma said. "He's always been a good boy."

Kody darted a look at Charlotte, found her accusing gaze on him. Knew she figured a "good boy" would not walk away from his daughter. She had no idea how difficult the decision had been. Leaving again would be even harder. He should never have come back.

"Kody?" Ma pulled his attention back to her. "Why don't you tell Charlotte your story."

"Go ahead and tell her, Ma. You know it better than I do." He chuckled. "I was too young to remember most of it."

"Very well." She turned to Charlotte. "One day more than twenty-one years ago, a girl came to our door, so sick and weak she couldn't talk. And about to have a baby. I helped her as best I could. It was all she could do to bring her little son into the world. She died without telling us her name or anything about herself. But the baby was healthy and strong. We've never been able to have children and thanked God for this little gift. We named him Dakota and he grew into the fine young man sitting in that chair."

Charlotte's eyes glistened. "That's beautiful. So all your life your parents have delighted in you." She choked up and couldn't continue.

Kody blinked. Yes, he was loved by his parents. He'd never doubted it. But the words, the accusations, the nasty comments of others were a raging flood covering his parents' love and pride with their dirty, muddy waters. He'd heard the story of his birth many times. As a child it made him feel special, a miracle gift to his ma and pa, but he grew up, discovered others looked upon his birth as less than a blessing. He learned to reason and as he did, he despised the details.

Charlotte widened her eyes and sent him a look full of something he could only describe as longing. Hadn't she once said something about wishing she had a mother like his? What a strange world. He envied her the way people accepted her, rushing to fill her order at the store and extending her little courtesies. It appeared she envied his loving parents. Seems like a person always wanted the things out of their reach.

He could tell her that what she wanted and envied him for might not satisfy what she seemed to ache for—a place where she felt accepted or...

He suddenly realized what she longed for—appreciation for who she was as a person.

"I've been working on a quilt," Ma said. "I'll finish it up and donate it to the cause."

Kody couldn't look at Ma. Avoided meeting Charlotte's gaze knowing the silent messages she'd be sending. She'd already accused him of robbing his parents of a granddaughter. But Ma and Pa must never know about Star.

Pa tried to get up from his big chair and Kody hurried to assist him. He helped Pa prepare for bed, then left Ma to tuck him in. "I'll say good night," she said as she headed out of the room.

Kody bid them both good night and hurried back to the front room. Somehow he had to explain his insight to Charlotte and make her understand how, if people didn't appreciate her, they were blind, ignorant and unworthy of her efforts to please them.

"I'm almost finished Star's dress. Do you think she'll like it?"

Kody faltered. Through no fault of her own, Star would face many of the same questions, doubts and prejudices Kody had never grown accustomed to. He had to stay away from her and give her a chance to be Indian and nothing else. She might also feel the same needs Charlotte did—a need for appreciation. Charlotte thought a parent's love would outweigh all those other things. But it didn't. He knew from experience.

"She'll like it just fine." He'd intended to sit down and talk to her. But now he wanted only to end this evening before his thoughts grew any more confused. "I'm going to see about finding work tomorrow."

"Can I help in any way?"

He chuckled at her eagerness. "Always trying to prove yourself indispensable, aren't you?" At the wounded look in her eyes, he wished he had enough brains to keep his thoughts to himself. She had no idea of the things causing him to say that. "You don't need so try so hard. Some people appreciate you just fine."

She opened her mouth, but not a sound escaped. Her gaze clung to his, expectant and unbelieving.

"I like you just fine." A poor way to say all he felt, but no other words came to his befuddled mind.

Twin spots of pink showed on her cheeks.

He'd embarrassed her. "You don't have to prove anything to me." The color in her face deepened. What was he trying to say? He rubbed his chin and tried again. "I appreciate your help. Making this dress for Star is a generous gesture. But, Charlotte, you don't have to work to gain my approval."

Her color heightened. She looked down, slowly folded the little dress, and got to her feet. "If you think I am doing this to make you like me, you are so wrong. I'm doing this because it's not fair how you're treating Star, and I want to show her that people can and do care about her." She pushed past him and headed for the stairs. "Even if her father doesn't."

He grabbed her elbow and stopped her escape. "You don't believe that. I do care about her. I'm trying to do what's best for her."

She turned slowly and fixed him with a hard stare. "And how do you expect to explain that to her? 'Cause I can guarantee soon or later she's going to want to know why her father left her."

"Charlotte, I don't want to argue about what I think is best for her."

"You're saying it's none of my business." She sighed. "You're right. I have no call to interfere." She climbed the stairs.

Kody ought to be grateful she'd given up the fight. But for some perverse reason it wasn't gratitude he felt. He stared at Charlotte's back. He didn't like this compliant, passive Charlotte.

> *Good little Charlotte, meek and mild*
> *Poke her hard and see her smile.*

He grinned. He knew one sure way to shake her from her meek and mild state. "Guess you'll just sit around and wait for Harry to send for you."

He stopped.

His grin widened as she lifted her chin.

Slowly she turned. "Kody Douglas, you are so wrong. I don't intend to do any such thing. I'll have the garments finished by the end of the week and then I expect you to take me to the reservation so I can deliver them. And I will prove to you that you need to take care of your daughter yourself." She spun around and strode down the hall.

Kody leaned back on his heels and chuckled softly. He loved to see Charlotte all feisty and ready to do battle. A sobering thought failed to quench his smile—her battle seemed to be always with him. It had been from the first. But somehow he didn't mind. Not that she had a chance of changing his mind. He'd already made that clear.

Kody pinned his note to the board next to the post-office door. "Willing to break horses for a fair price. Buck 'em out or gentle train them. Never been thrown."

A lanky cowboy sidled up to him and peered at the notice. "Never been throwed, huh? You ought to go by the Cartwell place. He's got a rank horse there. He's promised twenty bucks to anyone who can ride him."

Twenty dollars would buy a pair of little shoes and add some to his travel fund. "Cartwell, you say? They the ranch back in the hills?"

"Cross the river and up the trail." He shifted to look at Kody more carefully.

Kody stiffened, hoping the man wasn't going to create a scene in the post office.

"Say, I'll bet you're Kody Douglas."

Kody looked the other man up and down. Tall, slightly bow-legged, with a twinkle in his blue eyes. "Do I know you?"

"Don't suppose you do. I married Bess Macleod. She told me about you. Jed Hawkes." He shoved out his hand.

Kody shook it. "Nice to meet you." What a pleasant change to be welcomed.

Jed pushed aside a couple of notices. "Old Lady Murphy is looking for a man again."

"The Widow Murphy? I can't believe she's still alive. I thought she was old as Methuselah when I was a kid." He read the notice aloud. "'Need hardworking man willing to stay a spell. Top wages. Bonuses.' She really pay top wages?"

"Hear she pays good but not many men willing to stay."

"Why's that?"

"She's mighty particular that things are done exactly as they've been done for the past fifty years. She don't hold much for letting the men have days off. And on top of it, she lives so far back it's a hard ride to town. Man ends up stuck there with little to amuse 'im. Most just don't stay."

Kody studied the notice. It sounded like his kind of place, except for one thing—he needed to be close to town so he could help with Pa's care and see his folks were doing okay.

And he wasn't averse to seeing more of little Miss Charlotte, especially when she wasn't meek and mild. After she left, after Pa was doing better…well, he wouldn't need a job, because he'd be on his way to Canada again.

Chapter Ten

Charlotte glanced to the backseat of the car at the boxes of supplies they carried. The shirt and two dresses were finished. They had turned out rather well, she thought. She hoped the Eaglefeather family would receive them gladly.

Kody borrowed his pa's car for this trip to the reservation. "Car's faster than horseback and I want to be back in good time."

They bounced along, breathing in dust and hot air. "Sure could use rain," Charlotte said. The reservation was in the hills beyond irrigation and bereft of any sort of advantage.

"Yup."

He sounded cheerful, almost pleased with life. And she couldn't figure out why. She'd warned him yet again she had one goal—to persuade him to be a father to his little girl. But rather than being annoyed or defensive, he seemed almost glad about it, which made her wonder if he was up to something. She shifted so she could study him, hoping to get a clue.

"What?" he asked.

"What what?"

"You're staring."

She jerked her attention back to the road. "Sorry."

"Did you want to ask something?"

"No. Well, now that you mention it…why are you being so pleasant about this?"

"About what?"

She didn't miss the flash of amusement in his eyes. "You know I intend to make you change you mind."

He chuckled. "As I already told you, that will be impossible." He waggled his eyebrows. "But it's kind of fun to see you try."

She flicked him a warning look. "You ain't seen nothin' yet."

He laughed and slapped the steering wheel. "Like I said…" He slowed as they passed a spindly group of trees. "Isn't that smoke?"

"Looks like someone has set up camp."

"They shouldn't leave a fire unattended."

She saw a flash and followed it. "Someone's

there." A face peeked around a rock. The man saw the car and ducked out of sight. She laughed. "It's Ratface. And there's Shorty trying to hide behind a tree."

"I expect they're up to no good."

"They sure have a lot of junk scattered about."

They passed the camp and Charlotte turned her attention back to the road.

"I don't like them hanging about," Kody said.

"At least they aren't bothering us."

He grunted. "I hope it stays that way."

For several days Charlotte had tried to think of convincing words to present to Kody, something to make him see how much Star needed him. She knew without a doubt how the child would feel as bits of truth came out, and they would. She had prayed for guidance. But they were only a few miles from their destination and still she had no idea what she should say. But if she didn't say something soon, she'd have to wait until after their visit.

"Where did you meet Star's mother?"

"On the reservation. Winnoa had been fathered by a soldier. She had light eyes and freckles and knew what it felt like to be an outcast. I guess we gravitated toward each other because of our common half-breed status."

"Winnoa. What a lovely name. So you married and lived on the reservation?"

His short burst of laughter rang with bitterness. "We ran away and got married and tried to find work with anyone who would hire me. One half-breed is bad enough. Two is more than most people want to deal with."

"Did Star's birth have anything to do with her death?" Maybe he blamed the baby and, despite his best intentions, that affected his attitude toward his daughter.

"No. She got some kind of infection and…" He shrugged.

So he didn't blame Star. Hesitantly she asked, "Did you take her to a doctor?"

"He couldn't do anything to help her."

She exhaled noisily. And he couldn't blame her death on a doctor who refused to treat a half-breed. "Did you love her very much?"

He grinned at her. "What I loved most about her was she was a half-breed like me. That's about all we had in common."

For some reason his statement made Charlotte grin so widely she looked out the side window to hide her face. Not that she had anything in common with him. Mentally she listed their differences: he had the love of parents, yet it didn't seem to count, whereas she would do anything to make Harry continue to love her; Kody claimed to have left the faith he'd embraced as a child, and she clung to it for dear life; she thought he should be involved as a father to Star, and he seemed to think he should pretend he wasn't her father; and most of all, he was headed for Canada and she waited for Harry to send for her.

Yet none of those facts stopped her from being glad neither of them meant to move on yet.

The reservation came into view. Kody pulled to a stop in front of the Eaglefeathers' home. John and Morning waved. Star sat contentedly in John's arms.

Charlotte turned to see if Kody's face revealed any emotion at seeing his daughter held by another man. She thought she caught a flash of surprise, which he quickly masked. He hesitated a heartbeat before he opened the door. She could only pray he'd begun to see what he stood to lose by pretending Star wasn't his daughter.

John reached Kody's side and shook his hand. "Welcome, my friend. Star, say hello to Kody and Miss Charlotte."

"Hello." She had such an innocent huskiness to her voice. "He here with that lady before. She like my baby."

Morning welcomed them, then Kody opened the back door. "We brought you a few things." He pulled out a box.

No one moved. Charlotte feared the gifts offended their pride.

"Allow me to do something while I can." Kody's gaze lingered on Star.

John nodded and Kody carried the box to the house.

Morning followed. "It is very generous of you, Kody." She rested her hand on his arm. "We accept." She paused. "I understand how you need to feel you give something." She examined the contents of the box—oatmeal, oats, flour, canned goods.

Kody didn't move. A casual observer might think he was watching Morning lift out the items, but Charlotte stood where she could see his face and saw he looked past Morning, his eyes bleak, empty. It was as if Morning's words sucked away his determination, his so-called good reasons, and left him with nothing to replace them.

He spun back to the car to get the second box.

John stood in his way. "I'll get it." He handed Star to Kody.

Charlotte felt his hesitation more than she saw it. For a moment she thought he would refuse, then Star leaned toward Kody and he had no choice but to raise his arms and take his daughter. Emotions raced across his face—resistance, then surprise, then pleasure, as Star stared into his face with intent concentration. "What do you see, little one?" he asked.

"You."

He laughed. "Am I okay?"

She nodded. "You okay."

"Why, thank you." Kody's voice deepened.

John returned with a box and stopped to look at the pair. Morning straightened to watch them. Charlotte guessed the other two were as aware as she was that something special took place before their eyes. Kody would deny it, but he certainly had to feel it.

He glanced up, saw her watching him. "Let's see what else we have."

Charlotte nodded, went to get her own parcel from the back and opened it. She handed the dress to Morning, the shirt to John.

John grinned widely. "Nice shirt."

"Thank you." Morning spoke softly, shyly.

"And for you, little miss." Charlotte held out the dress, anxious to see Star's reaction.

Star's eyes grew wide. "For me?" She demanded to be put down. Kody did so, reluctantly, Charlotte thought, and kept his hands at her back until she balanced on her uneven legs. She held the dress before her. "Look, Momma. Just for me." Then she folded it into a rough bundle and pressed it to her chest.

Charlotte blinked back tears. She dared not look at Kody.

She had one more thing to give Star. A rag doll. Mrs. Douglas made them for Christmas gifts for the Sunday school. She'd helped Charlotte make this one. Charlotte had given the doll black yarn hair and braided it. She'd made dark brown eyes, rather than black, to match Star's. She'd made a little dress out of scraps from Star's dress.

She held the doll out to Star.

"Ooh, a new baby." Star handed her dress to Kody so she could take the doll. She examined it carefully, then sighed and cradled it close. "I love my baby. I love her forever."

"What do you say, Star?" Morning prompted her.

Star turned to Charlotte. "I love you very, very much."

Charlotte smiled even as her eyes filled with tears. What a precious child.

Star turned to Kody. "I love you very, very much, too."

Kody looked as if someone had put him through the wringer and hung him to dry.

"You should say, 'Thank you,'" Morning corrected.

Charlotte laughed. "That's better than a thank-you."

Kody turned away and stared out at the dry hills.

Charlotte took a step toward him, but Morning

stopped her. "You know about…?" She dipped her head toward Star.

"I know."

"That is good. But it is best to let Kody work things out in his own way."

Charlotte nodded and allowed Morning to lead her to the house, where she helped prepare lunch. However, she had no intention of sitting around waiting for Kody to do things in his own way. Because his way meant riding away from this special child.

They sat in the shade of the little house and ate a simple meal, drank copious amounts of tea and visited.

Star played at their feet, enjoying her new doll. She took the dress off and wrapped the doll in a scrap of material, then dressed it again. She examined the doll's feet for several minutes until Charlotte wondered if she should do something.

She turned her attention to Kody, who couldn't seem to stop watching the child. And she prayed he would be moved to reconsider his decision.

"Too bad about your foot," Star murmured to the doll.

Charlotte shifted her gaze back to Star. The impact of what the little girl had done would have knocked Charlotte backward if she wasn't sitting pressed to the wall. Instead, the sight hit her with the force of a dust storm, sucking at her lungs, stinging her eyes, echoing in her brain with the power of thunder over her head, reverberating through her with resounding waves.

Star had tied one cloth foot of the doll back with a thread. She cuddled the doll for a moment, making soothing noises. "It doesn't matter. I love you and you can still walk." She walked the doll around her in a limp that couldn't be disguised or explained away.

The wind made a sighing sound around the cabin, pulled at Charlotte's hair and tugged her scalp. The sun beat brittle light around them, flashing bright lights in Star's dark hair, drawing sharp angles across her face, giving her an older, more mature, more careworn look.

Charlotte ached to jump up and break the thread crippling the doll, but her limbs refused to do her bidding. She sat riveted to her perch.

"I fix it for you," Star said, and broke the thread, freeing the bent foot. "See, all better." In her hands, the doll danced and jumped.

Charlotte sucked in the hot air, heavy with so much sorrow, so much unnecessary pain. This child was made for loving even if her foot couldn't be fixed. Certainly John and Morning loved her unconditionally. Otherwise she wouldn't be such a happy, outgoing child. But she deserved more. The love of grandparents who would dote on this child. The love of her only living parent to carry her through the tough times ahead.

She shifted her gaze away from the wonder and pain and amazement of Star to Kody. An expert at masking his emotions, he hadn't been able to hide the pain of seeing Star act out the truth of her crippled foot. His eyes were wide, darker than the blackest of night. His mouth pulled to a hard line.

How could he pretend this child didn't need him? How long before her sweet innocence turned sour? About as long as it took her to overhear some of the remarks already said regarding her. About as long as it took for her to realize she'd been abandoned. How could Kody not see how she would feel?

Charlotte shook her head. There had to be a way she could convince him to reconsider his decision and save such needless pain.

Star struggled to her feet. Watching her limp toward Morning on her crooked foot filled Charlotte with fresh, pulsating pain.

Star leaned against Morning's knees. "Jesus will make my leg better when I see Him." She nodded, her eyes questioning.

Morning brushed her hand over Star's head. "In heaven you will run and jump like a deer." Her voice was soft and reassuring.

Star nodded. "I like that."

Kody watched Star, as did Charlotte. As the child moved away, he shifted. Their gazes brushed and stalled. She saw the tightness around his eyes, the way he pulled his mouth in as if he could contain his feelings, perhaps even deny them.

She'd hoped for, prayed for, something to change his mind, but she hadn't hoped for the pain she saw etched in his face. His pain became her pain, knifing into her heart with cruel abandon. She pressed her palm to her chest as if she could end it. She lifted her other hand toward Kody, wanting to end his suffering.

He sucked in a noisy gust of air, blinked, and suddenly his mask fell into place again, his eyes grew cool and indifferent, his mouth a mocking smile.

But she knew what she'd seen.

Chapter Eleven

Kody patted his pocket. He'd been to the Cartwell ranch. He'd clung to the back of that rank horse until they both knew he couldn't be thrown. He'd earned the twenty bucks. His first stop—the post office, where he intended to order those special shoes for Star.

Thinking of Star, he squinted, held his breath, preparing for the avalanche of emotion to thunder through him. There'd been too many deluges in the past three days to count. They'd started as he watched Star play with her doll, tying one foot back and then freeing it. The first avalanche almost swept him off his feet, literally. He would have given his own limbs if they could have fixed hers.

The second came hard on its heels when she'd gone to Morning wanting reassurance she would walk and run in heaven. Why should she have to wait until then to be free? He vowed he would earn money and order those shoes as quickly as humanly possible. He wanted to do more, but some things were out of the world of possibility. Charlotte declared she would pray for a miracle. He knew she didn't mean only Star's foot. He wished he believed in miracles as readily as Charlotte did. Right now he'd give his right arm for one.

He couldn't stop his thoughts from returning to another avalanche. Something grabbed his heart and squeezed it cruelly as he remembered Star's words: "I love you very, very much." He wished he could hear those words every day of his life. Just wasn't possible. Although the words twisted his gut, their sweetness soothed the sting.

He slowed his steps, waiting for the roar of emotions to pass before he entered the post office. One thing he appreciated, Charlotte hadn't mentioned the incident on the trip home. He couldn't have handled her pointing out how much Star needed him. He pretty much figured he'd end up telling her he needed the child even more than she needed him. He wanted to be the one to encourage Star through each day, to tell her he loved her very much and her crooked foot only made him love her more. He wanted to hear her sweet words of love every day he lived. But acknowledging his love for her did not change one thing—she would be better off raised as an Indian than facing rejection in a white world. Or worse, sharing his half-breed world, fitting with neither race.

He'd been glad of Charlotte's quiet presence beside him on the trip back to town, and when she squeezed his arm, he gripped the steering wheel extra hard to stop himself from reaching for her. He wanted to hold her close and breathe in the sweet, fresh scent of her hair and skin, like the breeze off the mountains on a spring day. He kept himself from opening his arms to her, but he couldn't stop the new cleft forming in his heart that let in the pure sunshine of her presence. She knew how it felt to be rejected. It made her sweet, kind and understanding. For the first time he felt safe with someone besides his parents and the Eaglefeathers.

He reached the post office and firmly pushed his distracting thoughts out of the way. He threw open the door and jerked to a halt.

Charlotte stood halfway across the room.

He hadn't seen her since yesterday when, glad of the excuse, he'd stayed home with Pa while Charlotte and Ma went to church. He'd left this morning before anyone else awoke.

She turned, saw him, and her eyes flared with

welcome. Her mouth curved in a smile, making him long for things not possible for a man like him—home and family and permanency.

"Hi." Her voice filled with the sound of happiness—he let himself think she was glad to see him.

He nodded and grinned. She indicated he should do his business first, so he asked for an envelope, addressed it and made out the money order for an amount to cover the cost of the shoes.

Charlotte stood close behind, watching. "I hope they help," she murmured.

"Me, too." His voice sounded thick and he cleared his throat.

"You want the mail?" Mr. Scofield asked.

"Sure thing."

Mr. Scofield handed him three thin envelopes. He checked them. Two were for Pa. The third for Miss Charlotte Porter. The expected letter from Harry? For a moment he thought of pretending it wasn't there. The minute she opened it she would be off to join her brother without a thought in any other direction. Belonging was more important to her than anything else. Certainly more than something as uncertain and bound to be full of rejection as staying with him would be.

No, he didn't mean him. He had other plans.

And even if he did mean her, he couldn't think of her being treated like a white squaw.

He handed her the letter.

"It's from Harry." She pressed it to her chest. "Finally."

Kody knew how she'd react—nothing mattered but rejoining Harry, the brother who didn't mind deserting her on the farm.

She stepped back to a corner by the window, carefully ran her thumbnail under the flap and pulled out one page. She looked inside the envelope and shook it.

"I thought he would send a money order."

She unfolded the page, torn from an old school scribbler, and read the letter aloud. "'We are in a tiny shack. Can't find work. You must wait. I will send for you at first opportunity.'" She gave a tiny cry of distress and read the letter again, her mouth silently repeating the words.

Kody stepped closer, aching to comfort her, assure her he didn't mind if she stayed around Favor for a while.

She folded the page, placed it carefully back in the envelope and pushed it into her pocket. "How could Harry simply abandon me? I haven't even been able to write and inform him I'm with your parents. For all he knows I've starved to death on poverty acres. The house could have fallen down around my head." She flung an angry look at Kody. "Maybe he hopes I've decided to marry Lother out of desperation." She shuddered. "If you'd turned out to be a scoundrel, I could be on my way to Canada without leaving a trace. But does Harry care? Apparently not. He didn't even ask how I was."

She pushed past Kody and stormed from the building.

Kody followed on her heels, hoping she didn't intend to do something foolish. He'd seen how her anger fueled her to do things she wouldn't normally consider.

"Charlotte—"

"Don't talk to me. I'm not in the mood." She headed down Main Street, then reconsidered and spun around.

He leaped out of her way.

"I do all I can do to please both him and Nellie. I run errands, do the dirty jobs, all—" she flung him an accusing look as if he was personally at fault "—without complaining. But does it count? No. I'm his sister. You'd think it would make me part of the family, but it doesn't seem to."

She made a sharp right and steamed onward. She drew in a long breath and slowed. "Sometimes it's mighty hard to see God's hand in these things."

They walked on at a slower pace, passing the newer houses.

"I told you about being sent to the Applebys."

He felt angry just thinking about how she'd been treated. "I gather it wasn't a happy experience for you."

"He had no right to send me away, but Nellie… Never mind. The reasons no longer matter. But I was a kid, a babe in the woods. I needed someone to protect me. I had no one." She stopped and fixed Kody with a look so full of pain and confusion that he took her hand and pulled her off the street into a little park. He led her to a bench and waited for her to sit, then dropped down beside her.

He wanted to hold her in his arms, make all the bad things go away, but he didn't know how she'd react to such a bold move. So he hesitantly took her hand and let out a tense breath when she gripped it.

"Jerrod, the oldest Appleby boy, eighteen years old, thought himself pretty special and so did his parents. What Jerrod wanted, Jerrod got. And when he decided he wanted me, they turned a blind eye. They had to see the way he watched me, how he made excuses to come into the kitchen when I was along. But who was I? Just a servant girl. His sister, Viola, was the only one who showed me any kindness. And she saw. She watched Jerrod and when he came to my bed one night, she followed him. She called her parents to confront him. But of course, he wasn't at fault. *I* was. They wanted to turn me into the street, but Viola took me to a friend and contacted Harry." Her voice filled with bitterness. "I'm surprised he came to get me."

"Let me guess. That's when Nellie had a baby."

"Yes. Ricky. But I didn't care why they'd let me come back. I was that glad to be safe." She squeezed his hand so hard he wondered where she got the strength.

The wind whined around the trees, carrying with it the never-ending supply of dust that stung Kody's cheeks. He lifted his face to the bite of each particle. He dared the wind to do more, cut his skin with its tiny, sharp weapons, shred it; he would let blood gush from each torn pore. Even that would not equal the way Charlotte's words tore at his insides. He hoped he'd meet Harry someday. His muscles clenched. Best for both of them if he never did.

Charlotte sighed and leaned back, still clinging to his hand. "You see, I know what it's like to be forsaken by your only living relative."

Her silent accusation iced his veins. He withdrew his hand. "How can you make this about Star? She's in a safe place. Morning and John love her."

"Yes, they do, but will it be enough when she discovers the truth, or at least cruel hints of it?"

"Why should she?"

"Let's see." She held up one finger. "First, everyone knows she isn't Morning's child." She held up another finger. "People can figure out who might be the parents by simple deduction. Or by gossip and guesswork." She held up a third finger. "As I'm sure you've noticed, she doesn't have Indian eyes."

"They're pretty dark."

She made a disbelieving sound.

He faced her squarely. "You also discovered what it's like for people not to accept you. It makes you afraid, vulnerable. It hurts."

She took his hand. "I'm sorry you've been hurt by what people say. But how can it turn you from your own child? She needs you. You need her."

He wanted to pull away from Charlotte. He hadn't meant himself when he said rejection hurt. He wanted to deny what she said. He couldn't. Neither could he escape the knowledge Morning and John might be able to give Star what he could not—a place where she'd be accepted. "She's safe with them. They would never send her away or put her in a position like Harry did to you."

Charlotte's shoulders sagged. "Yes, at least she'll be safe."

Kody's anger fled. "You no longer need Harry to keep you safe." He ached to promise her he would be willing to do it, but he couldn't. He didn't plan to stay. "Besides—" he started to grin "—you're no longer a child and quite capable of taking care of yourself. Haven't you proved it several times since Harry left? Maybe it's served a good purpose—you have learned how strong you are."

Her gaze clung to him as if seeking truth and reassurance from him.

He smiled, quite willing to give her whatever she needed.

Slowly, the tension in her face faded. "I have done some surprising things since I met you." Her eyes widened. "I guess I have you to blame." Her voice dropped to a whisper. "Or should I thank you?"

"You can thank me if you want." He studied her lips and thought of a time-honored way of expressing thanks. He jerked his attention back to something he needed to say. If he could only remember what it was. Oh, yeah. "But you don't need me to goad you into being strong. That's what you are and you need to realize it."

She searched his face. Her gaze delved deep into his eyes. "You might not like me strong, ready to defend and protect."

He wondered if her cheek was as smooth as he imagined and touched it. His heart leaped to his fingertips at the warm, soft texture. Slowly, giving her lots of chance to duck away, he lowered his head and touched her lips in the softest form of a kiss.

A pair of women passed. One tsked loudly. "Did you see that?" she proclaimed in a loud whisper. "Some people have no decency. You expect it from his sort, but her?" She sniffed loud enough to suck the dust from a thirty-foot radius.

Kody jerked back. He would have bolted to his feet, but Charlotte grabbed his hand. She grinned at him. "Didn't you just point out I need no protecting? I'm a strong person, remember?"

She rose slowly, seemingly unaffected by the way the women glanced over their shoulders, and she held his hand firmly. He could have easily broken away if he tried. He didn't.

"Where are we going?" Charlotte asked. She seemed happy in spite of her letter from Harry.

Kody hoped he might have something to do with it. At his invitation, after supper they left Ma reading to Pa in the front room and headed outside for a walk. "Do you want to see where I used to play?"

"Sure"

He'd hardly been able to keep his eyes off her throughout the meal and had to force himself to pay attention to Ma as she told how Pa walked from the bedroom without any help. He was glad Pa showed improvement, but it paled in comparison to the idea of spending time with Charlotte.

He took her hand, liking how it fit perfectly into his palm, liking how she moved closer to his side as they walked down the alley. They cut across an empty lot and were soon out of town. Half a mile later he helped her up a steep hill to a rugged crop of rocks. "One of my favorite places to play when I was a kid."

She looked about, then flashed a smile that warmed him deep inside. "What did you play?"

"Depends if I was alone or with a friend." He'd almost forgotten those happy times, allowed them to be swallowed up by the other stuff—the cruel remarks, the whispers not meant to be secret and his growing resentment.

"What did you play alone?"

"I would make little hideouts in the rocks and pretend to be a real Indian." He led her to a hollowed-out spot. "See, here's one of the places. Sometimes Ma even let me spend the night. That was great. I'd lie on my back staring at the stars and thinking."

She leaned against a nearby rock and watched him poke through the dirt. "What did you think about?"

"Mostly about what it would have been like to be the first man to see this place, how big the ocean is, what makes the stars twinkle. Does God love everyone the same—" He stopped. He hadn't meant to say the last part, but now that he had, he wondered if Charlotte would try to answer it.

"I've wondered, too, and I've decided He loves everyone, but some people see more of it."

"What do you mean?"

"I think people who have hard things to deal with know more about God's love, don't you?"

Kody stared at her. He wasn't sure he agreed with her. In his case, had his difficulties turned him to God? No, they'd turned him away. But Charlotte…

"I guess I'd have to say it seems to have made you cling to God."

She smiled so serenely it caressed his heart just watching her. Something sweet and good, something gentle and healing, slipped into his heart. "I know He loves me but no more or less than He loves you."

He believed her. For the first time in years, Kody felt as if God cared about him. Not that it changed anything. People would still treat him the same. But rather than spoil the moment by pointing out the unchangeable realities of life, he turned the talk to other things. "My friends and I loved to play hide-and-seek or—" he slanted her a look, wanting to see her reaction "—cowboys and Indians. Guess who had to fight not to be the Indian?"

She blinked as if having trouble following his change of subject, then slowly her eyes widened and she laughed. "I can't imagine who got picked to be the Indian. I suppose the most unruly friend."

He laughed. "I was always a good kid, but it didn't make any difference. I still had to be the Indian. Most times I didn't mind. I liked sneaking up on them and scaring them. I even tried to scalp Tommy Tompson once."

She looked suitably shocked. "You didn't."

"With a pretend knife."

She laughed. "It sounds like you had a lot of fun as a kid."

Telling Charlotte about those happy times filled him with sweet pleasure. "I did. Didn't you?"

"My father died when I was a baby and Harry left home to work when I was only eight, so Mother and I were alone. As long as I can remember, Mother was sick. I had little time for play. I learned early to help out as much as I could."

"Maybe it's time you had a little fun."

She looked vaguely uninterested.

"You *are* familiar with the idea, aren't you?"

"Of course."

Suddenly he dashed behind some rocks to a place he remembered hiding. The place didn't quite accommodate his size anymore, but he tucked himself deep into the crevice and waited. He didn't have to wait long.

"Kody, where are you?"

"Find me," he growled deep in his throat.

"Kody. Stop it."

"It's called play," he called, and then hunkered down further as he heard her start around the rocks.

"Where are you?" she called, drawing closer.

He hoped she couldn't see him.

She called again, closer, called yet again, this time just inches away. Unless she turned she could pass by and not see him. She paused. "Kody. This isn't funny."

He hadn't enjoyed anything this much in a long time. Maybe he was the one who'd forgotten how to play. He counted—one, two, three—and as she took another step, leaped out with a yell rivaling any uttered by an Indian, imagined or real.

She screamed and took off like a shot.

"Yiiiie, yiiie, yiii!" He raced after her.

She glanced back, saw him and turned around. "That's not funny. You scared me out of ten years."

He bent over his knees, laughing. "It was priceless."

"Why you…" She began a measured stalk toward him.

Still chuckling, he straightened, tensed and when she almost reached him, jumped away.

She broke into a run, trying to catch him.

He darted back and forth, taunting her, tempting her to catch him before he ducked away.

She stopped, plucked a blade of grass, examined it as she edged toward him, pretending the grass held her attention, trying to make him think she didn't want to catch him, but he wasn't fooled and leaped away as she lunged for him. His foot caught on a rock and with a yell, he fell on his back.

She pounced, pressing her hands to his chest. "Serves you right, you crazy man."

He didn't move to escape. Instead, he locked eyes with her. Her gaze went on and on. Beyond his past, over his feelings of inadequacy, straight to the cracks and scars on his heart, and in that moment, by some spiritual miracle, they began to heal.

"You caught me," he whispered, meaning far more than pinning him to the ground.

"I'm trying to decide what to do with you."

"I can tell you."

"Really?"

"This." He cupped her head and lifted his head to meet her mouth with his.

He felt her surprise and then a quiet yielding. Then he pulled back and looked into eyes full of dark emotion. He wished he could believe it to be acceptance and caring, when most likely it was nothing more than surprise at his boldness. He'd kissed her twice in one day. And she'd let him. He guessed that meant something, thought he couldn't say for sure what. Nor what he wanted it to mean. This was getting way too complicated.

She sat back on her heels, looking out over the hills, but didn't say anything.

Glad not to have to deal with his confusion, he scrambled up and sat beside her, his legs stretched out on the brittle grass. The sun sank low in the west. The air, foggy with dust, turned pink. He waited for her to speak, wondering if she would scold him or…

He wouldn't let himself dream of other possibilities. Yet all the reasons he could hope flashed through his mind. She never seemed to notice he had Indian blood in him until he reminded her. Could it be possible? His heart rattled against his ribs like a rock tossed by turbulent water. He could love this woman if he let himself. The realization hit him like a full-force gale, sucking away his breath, turning his insides into a whirlwind of warm, delightful thoughts—the joy of sharing every moment with her, the fun of teasing and making her laugh, the pleasure of seeing her grow feisty and defensive…

"It's a pretty evening," she said. "I wish life could always be like this—soft and pleasant."

"Huh." Not much he could say to something like that, because wishing didn't change the harsh realities of life—something he would do well to remember.

He pushed to his feet, dismissing his delightful, totally unrealistic dreams. "We better get back." For a few delicious moments, he'd let himself think—but even if she did care about him he knew the censure she'd face if she acknowledged it. The best thing he could do was get himself out of this town as fast as possible and ride for Canada like he was driven by the relentless wind.

Only, he had to see Star with her new shoes first.

He had to make sure Pa would be able to take care of himself.

He wanted to enjoy a few more days of Charlotte's company.

Chapter Twelve

Martha, as Mrs. Douglas had insisted she be called, said she needed nothing more done. The walls were scrubbed, the windows gleamed and a batch of rhubarb jam lined a shelf in the cellar.

Charlotte left the house and headed toward the park where she and Kody had sat a few days ago. The day he told her she was a strong woman, the day he kissed her.

She needed to think, figure out what it all meant. She sat on the bench and prayed. *God, I think I love Kody, but I'm confused. I don't know if it's real or if it's returned. Keep me from dong anything foolish.*

He thinks I'm strong.

Could it be possible? She'd been so busy trying to please she hadn't thought of anything else. Until

Harry left her, she'd gladly, willingly, let him or Nellie dictate her every move. She chuckled, thinking it had been fun to make some of her own decisions and even exert a little defiance. She'd managed to scare off Ratface and Shorty. For a moment she wondered if they'd moved on, then she forgot the pair as she cherished the memory of how she and Kody had played a game of tag ending in a kiss.

Her feelings for Kody were so fresh and unfamiliar she could hardly think what they meant. She only knew she felt safe with him in a way completely different from the way she felt with Harry. She trusted Kody. He would always be honest and sincere. Even when he didn't want to be. Even when she didn't want to hear what he had to say because she preferred not to face the truth.

But was she simply looking for someone to replace Harry?

It was all so convoluted and confusing.

She could only again pray that God would guide her and keep her from being foolish.

She left the park, but took her troubling thoughts with her as she walked the streets of Favor. Eventually she ended up in one of the stores. She bent over a display case to admire a tiny hand mirror. She wished she had the money to purchase it for Star. The child got so much pleasure out of simple things. She imagined her enjoying the little mirror.

She left off staring at the mirror and wandered around the store, aimless and bored. She wasn't used to having nothing to do. But she recognized her restlessness went deeper than boredom. Kody rode off early every day, gone to some ranch to break horses. She'd seen men ride wild horses to a standstill. Or more often, get tossed to the ground trying. Some suffered more than surface injuries. She tried not to think of Kody being hurt.

But until he returned each evening, she missed him and worried about him.

She left the store and sauntered over to the post office to ask for the mail. She stopped to poke through the notices on the bulletin board, not looking for anything, simply passing time.

A woman hurried through the door and over to the wicket. "Give me my mail, Matt."

"On your way to the hospital, are you?"

"I am. I hadn't expected to work today, but Matron practically begged me to come in. We're run off our feet with cases of dust pneumonia. We could sure use some help."

Charlotte turned to see who spoke. The woman appeared to be in her thirties and wore a crisp white uniform and white cap with stiff, starched wings. Could they use *her?* It would be nice to be needed again. She drew in a deep, courage-giving breath and approached the woman. "What kind of help do you need?"

The woman looked her up and down with sharp eyes, taking in every detail. "Are you volunteering?"

"Could I? I mean, I have no nursing experience."

"Can you run and fetch? Follow orders?"

"As well as most, better than some." Something about this woman made Charlotte speak briskly.

"Then go down to the hospital and ask to speak to Matron Morrow. Tell her Helen Chester sent you. And be prepared to start work immediately. Wear a big apron and pin your hair up." Mrs. Chester smiled. "You'll be welcomed with open arms. Of course, you'll be paid a fair wage."

"I'll be there as soon as I deliver the mail to the Douglases."

"You're living with them?"

Charlotte nodded. "For now." For how long she didn't dare venture a guess.

Mrs. Chester's smile widened. "They're good folk. Anyone associated with them needs no other recommendation. Now hurry. I can use your help."

Charlotte dashed from the building and hurried up the street. Breathless by the time she reached the Douglas home, she clattered into the house, raced upstairs and into the sewing room, where she knew Martha would be.

Martha looked up, startled by her rushed entrance. "Charlotte, what is it?"

"I have a job." She told of her conversation with Mrs. Chester. "I guess I'm going to need one if I have to support myself."

"You'll always be welcome here."

"I know." She also knew how desperately short of cash Martha and Leland were. "I appreciate it, but I'll feel better contributing something."

She changed into a clean cotton dress Nellie had given her when she gained weight with Mandy. It wasn't material Charlotte would have chosen. The pale pink color looked faded even when new, the flowers unnatural. Nellie made the dress plain as bread, but Charlotte had prettied it up with a daisy stitch around the color. According to Mrs. Chester's instructions, she pinned her hair back and twisted it into a little bun. She borrowed a big white apron from Martha. Not certain how long she'd be there or what arrangements had been made for the staff to eat, she packed a small lunch and set off. From the bottom of her stomach crept an uneasy feeling she tried to ignore. She'd never spent any time in a hospital. Could she handle the sight of so many sick people?

Matron Morrow greeted her as if expecting her.

"Nurse Chester said you might show up. You look sturdy enough. Now let me tell you what you will encounter. Most of our patients right now are here with dust pneumonia. Many are quietly struggling to avoid the inevitable. We do all we can to ease their suffering. Others, thank God, are recovering."

Charlotte tried not to think of the despair of those dying and vowed she would do all she could to help both them and the recovering ones. "What do you want me to do?"

"Assist the weaker ones. Get them to eat or drink if you can. Take water to the thirsty. I don't think you'll have any trouble keeping busy if you are at all industrious."

Charlotte decided then and there she would prove to Matron Morrow and every nurse on the staff how useful she could be. Matron led her down the hall and into the wards. The whole building rattled with coughing—loud, hacking coughs, as well as gasping, struggling ones. Charlotte remembered the lung-deep irritation of breathing in too much dust and longed to be able to ease each sufferer.

She stepped into the women's ward and noticed that the patients were thin, pale and out of breath. Most were elderly. Or mere children. Within minutes she was busy. She carried water to everyone. She spent an hour rubbing the back of a small boy while his parents sat on two metal chairs, their feelings so clear in their eyes—fear, dread, worry and a tiny shred of hope their child would survive.

She paused at noon, following Nurse Chester's instructions to join the nurses in the kitchen. Cook presented them with steaming cups of coffee while the nurses opened their sacks of food. Charlotte gratefully opened the lunch she'd packed.

Matron's prediction proved right. The afternoon passed so quickly Charlotte could hardly believe it when one of the nurses tapped her on the shoulder. "It's time to go home."

Matron stepped out of her office. "Can we count on you tomorrow morning?"

"If you want me." She'd scurried around from patient to patient, she'd helped measure out medications, she'd tried to comfort an old, old man so wrinkled and shrunken he might have been a hundred. Only, he comforted her. "Don't worry about the drought and dust—every day means we're a day closer to it raining." Charlotte laughed at his philosophy.

"You did well," Matron said. "I'll be glad to see you regularly."

Although her feet hurt clear up to her knees and weariness swept over her, Charlotte reveled in Matron's praise as she headed home. For the first time in ages she'd done something of significance.

Her footsteps slowed. This was the *first* time she'd done something *she'd* decided to do, and it felt good right down to the soles of her very sore feet.

Martha had supper prepared when Charlotte got back, and guilt swept away some of her joy. She rushed forward. "I'm sorry I wasn't here to help."

Kody came into the house in time to hear Charlotte's apology. He quirked an eyebrow and his silent look asked many questions.

She could barely contain her excitement. She wanted to tell him, tell them all, how much she enjoyed her new job, but first she had to make sure she did her share of the work here. "Next time wait until I get home"

Martha fluttered a hand at her. "I can manage to prepare a meal. You sit down and put your feet up."

But Charlotte could not. She helped carry the bowls of vegetables to the table.

Leland waited for everyone to be seated, then lifted a hand. "I will pray." His words slurred, he nevertheless managed a quiet, heartfelt prayer full of gratitude. "Lord of all creation, You have made each of us. You have blessed us. Thank you. Amen."

Charlotte glanced at Kody, wondering if he shared Leland's gratitude. He smiled, and the smile fell into her heart with an unexpected burst of pleasure. She ducked her head. How silly to think she might be part of the reason he seemed happy. Yet she hoped…

"I got a job," she said.

"Good for you. Who had the good sense to hire you?"

His ready approval pleased her more than she cared to admit. "I'm an aide at the hospital."

Over the meal she told them about her work. She repeated the old man's remarks about every day of drought being closer to the end of it, and everyone laughed. "I'm to go back tomorrow." She stopped and looked at Martha. "Of course, if you need me—"

Martha laughed. "You go to work. It's the best thing for you."

"She's right," Kody said. "This is just what you need to get your mind off waiting for life to happen."

He probably meant his words to be encouraging, but they stung. Did he think she sat around waiting? No. She worked while she waited. She grinned, silently acknowledging the truth of his words.

"They need strong people like you to help with the sick."

His reminder that he thought her strong made her sit taller. "I enjoy the work."

They exchanged quick smiles, then she ducked

away before Martha and Leland could think her too bold with their son.

"How did your day go?" she asked of everyone, but looked at Kody, wanting to hear what he'd done since she last saw him. Seems Leland and Martha felt the same, as they turned to him and waited for his answer.

"Nothing exciting about my day. Broke a few horses. Saw a baby hawk learning to fly. Outrode a dust storm." He said it with such calm, bored, flat tones that for a minute Charlotte thought he might have been reading a list of supplies. She saw the twinkle in his eye at the same time as she realized how out of the ordinary the events had been, and she laughed.

Leland and Martha laughed, too.

Kody grinned and seemed pleased he'd amused them.

Charlotte worked ten days before she got a day off. She picked up her first pay and before she headed home, stopped at the store to buy the mirror she'd admired.

Kody continued to work on nearby ranches, mostly breaking horses but doing odd jobs, as well. "Anything to make a few bucks."

She didn't ask what he planned to do with the money—it wasn't any of her business—but she knew it would finance his Canada trip. He never said anything to suggest he'd changed his mind. She knew he waited for the shoes for Star, and hung about to help Leland. But every day Leland grew stronger, and once the shoes came…

What would keep him there after that?

How could she hope she might be a reason for him to stay? Sure, they found more and more excuses to spend time together. She very much enjoyed walking and talking with him, and sharing stories after Martha and Leland went to bed. But was it enough to convince him to abandon his plan to head to Canada?

She glanced at the package she carried. She'd made little progress toward convincing him to become Star's father. To her shame, she'd been distracted with her own interests. Her work at the hospital was both satisfying and demanding.

A sense of urgency made her walk faster. She didn't know how much time she had left to accomplish her goal. She only knew she didn't dare waste another minute.

Kody returned for the evening meal. When she'd helped clean up afterward, he asked if she wanted to go with him to check on the horses kept in the small pen in the back of the yard. He rode Sam almost everywhere he went and threw out some feed for Blackie before he left each morning.

She agreed to accompany him, reminding herself she must use this opportunity to work on him about Star.

They leaned on the top rail of the fence. "I suppose we ought to sell Blackie," Kody said. "She's nothing but a hay burner."

"I hate to see her go." The horse had been so patient with Charlotte on the ride to Favor.

"It's not like anyone rides her."

"I might decide to."

"What for?"

"Something to do."

"Aren't you pretty busy with the hospital and all?"

"Didn't you remind me the other day that a person should play, too?"

His head jerked up and their gazes locked. "Showed you how, too." His voice seemed husky.

She couldn't look away from his black eyes. She couldn't get a sound past her constricted throat. Yes, she'd enjoyed the kiss. Even more, she'd been thrilled to think he cared about her, had forgotten for just a few minutes he was both Indian and white and yet neither, remembered only he was a man and she was a woman and something good and strong and right had been growing between them since he'd walked into Harry's house in the middle of a dust storm. He'd blown

her right out of her complacent frame of mind as
cleanly as the wind swept bare the dried-out
prairie.

"You've been showing me lots of things." She
finally managed to squeeze out the words.

He looked deep into her eyes, searching past her
words, past her smile to something deeper, something she wasn't sure she wanted to expose. "Like
what?" he asked.

"How to be strong. I'm liking it."

"You would have discovered it yourself
sooner or later."

"Maybe." She hovered between taking another
step toward what he thought she could be, and
clinging to his strength. Yet neither was safe.
Being independent felt good but scared her. She
was used to someone else taking care of problems.
However, leaning on him would be futile. He'd
ride out as quickly as Harry had when he finished
here. That brought her sharply back to her real
purpose for wanting to talk to Kody alone. She'd
decided coming directly at the subject of Star only
caused him to throw up instant, automatic resistance. So she would try something indirect.

She knew he'd visited the reservation several
times since she'd been there last—surely a
good sign. "Shouldn't those shoes have been
here by now?"

"They have to be specially made. John gave me an outline of her feet to send with the order. I suppose it takes time."

"I wonder if you'd give me a ride out to the reservation so I can give Star a little present."

"Sure. I planned to go tomorrow, anyway."

Chapter Thirteen

Kody again borrowed Pa's car to drive to the reservation. The sun shone with brittle determination. But it only made Kody smile. "One day closer to rain," he murmured, reminding Charlotte of the old man in the hospital.

"One more day of God's blessing."

He didn't argue. Seems God had been giving Kody many gifts lately, which made him nervous, suspicious, cautious. He wondered when the rug would be yanked out from under him.

But Charlotte seemed bent on itemizing her blessings. "I am so grateful for my job. I love the work. And your father is getting better every day. I'm sure if I look around I can think of more things to rejoice about."

He glanced at her, saw the way her eyes

caressed him, wondered if she counted him among the things she was grateful for. Her cheeks blossomed pink and then she jerked her attention to something out the window. He'd been staring, drinking in her smile and gentle spirit. He had no right to allow himself such thoughts. Not that he didn't like to believe she might return his feelings of welcome, connection, acceptance, but love? No way. He couldn't allow himself to love her. Even as he couldn't admit he was Star's father. Because nothing changed. Nothing ever changed. It never would. He would forever remain a half-breed, hated by most of the whites because he was too Indian, shunned by most of the Indians because he was too white. And anyone who loved him got the same cold shoulder from others. He would never do that to Charlotte. Yet he smiled, recalling how she'd purposely ignored the women in the park on that day when he'd admitted he had very deep feelings for her, when he'd kissed her and reveled in her acceptance. For a few delicious moments, he'd let himself think about what it would be like…

He knew better than to even think about it.

He shifted the conversation to Pa's announcement he intended to go to church tomorrow. "I expect next thing we know Pa will be wanting to start preaching again."

Charlotte chuckled. "Your mother says he's finally started to fight back from this stroke, and now she wonders if it isn't as bad as having him lie there and do nothing. She said she doesn't dare leave the house because the minute she does, he tries to do something she doesn't think he should. Yesterday he climbed the stairs. She came home to find him sitting in the rocker in her sewing room. Said she almost had a heart attack."

They laughed, their eyes connecting with shared pleasure and amusement.

"Its good to see Pa more like his old self."

"He's been reading the Bible and making notes, but he complains to Martha he can't read his own writing anymore. He asked her to make notes for him. She refused. 'If I do,' she said, 'the next thing, you'll be wanting me to hold you up while you stand at the pulpit.'"

Again they laughed.

"He'll be standing there on his own before we know it if I know my pa."

"Are you going to accompany him to church tomorrow?"

Pa had asked him, but Kody murmured something about having an important task to take care of.

"Do you plan to give him some weak excuse?"

He shot her a look. "Sometimes I think I liked you better complacent and submissive."

She lifted her chin. "Well, thanks to you, I'm not anymore."

"Me?"

"Yes, you. You stomped into my safe little house and literally forced me to leave."

He laughed. "How can you call that a safe place?"

"Because it was familiar and where Harry told me to wait."

Harry! Kody had no use for the man. How could he ride off and leave the woman in his charge? Kody's thoughts did a sudden turn. But leaving Star with Morning and John was not the same. Not even close.

Thankfully they arrived at the Eaglefeathers', sparing him having to argue further with himself or answer the challenge in Charlotte's eyes.

He'd brought more supplies, including some tinned beef. Charlotte and Morning made a stew with it. Charlotte waited until they sat back with cups of tea, helping themselves to biscuits from a tin he'd brought, before she got the package from the car.

"Star, this is for you."

Star held the unopened parcel, her eyes sparkling. "Oh, goody! Just what I always wanted."

The adults laughed.

Kody said, "Shouldn't you open it first and see what it is?"

Star carefully pulled the ends of the bow and removed the string. She scrunched it into a bundle and handed it to Morning. "I save it."

"I'll put in a safe place."

Star folded back the paper. The sun flashed in the mirror and she jerked back, looking frightened.

Charlotte knelt at her side. "It's a mirror. You look in it and see yourself." She held it to her face first and patted her hair. Then turned it to Star. "See."

Star stared openmouthed, then took the mirror. She touched her hair. Made faces and giggled.

Kody laughed at her antics. And he pushed away the pain he would never quite get used to, even though he knew he did the right thing in leaving her here.

He joined the conversation, but kept his eyes on Star. She struggled to her feet and hobbled toward him. He prayed God would use those special shoes to straighten her foot. He didn't even bother to question why he felt he would pray for someone else but not himself.

Star leaned her bony elbows on his knees. Although it hurt, he welcomed it. When he was alone in Canada, he would touch those twin spots and remember her looking up at him like this.

She held the mirror for him to look into. Then

she pulled it away and looked into his eyes so demandingly he almost shifted his gaze. "Eyes black," she announced, and moved to John, where she did the same thing.

"Eyes black," she said, and moved to Morning's knees. "Eyes black," she announced again, then shifted to Charlotte's knees. She looked into Charlotte's face a long time. "Light eyes."

She sat down in the middle of the yard again and looked into the mirror. "Light eyes." She lay the mirror down. "I get baby." She hobbled into the small house.

Kody's insides curled like an angry fist. Charlotte was right. Star already recognized she was different.

"Some of the children call her Light Eyes," John murmured.

Kody's fists balled. His shoulder muscles tensed. Was his daughter to face prejudice even here? Because of something she couldn't help or change? He leaned forward to the balls of his feet. He wanted to run. But where would he run? To Canada? Even there he would not be able to escape the pain this knowledge gave him.

"They are not unkind," John said, as if suspecting Kody's fear. "Just stating a fact."

Slowly the tension seeped from Kody's limbs, leaving him feeling beaten and chewed.

He felt Charlotte's gaze on him but couldn't look at her. She would see his pain. She would guess his fears and use them to fuel her arguments.

Star returned with her rag doll and played happily for the rest of the afternoon. Two black-eyed girls about Star's age came over and squatted beside her. Star let them play with the mirror and shared her doll. The three of them giggled together like any little girls would.

Kody smiled. She was accepted here, had friends. He was right to leave her. Even if it hurt all the way to the depths of his marrow and to the ends of every nerve in his body.

Later he held the car door for Charlotte as they prepared to leave. She gave him a long, demanding look, which he ignored. She would have something to say about the afternoon on the ride home, but he figured if he had his say first, she wouldn't get a chance to poke at his pain.

"I remember when I was young," he began, determined to show Charlotte how prevailing prejudice was, even toward children, hoping it would silence her campaign to make him agree otherwise. "Ma had some ladies over for tea. I remember the little cakes they had and how they all managed to hold tiny little cups so daintily. They sat in the front room discussing some missionary project. I recall the door being open to let in a breeze, and I sat by it, looking outside, wishing I could be out there running and playing, but Ma insisted I dress up like a little man and sit through the visit. I watched a tall Indian walking down the street and thought how proud he seemed. His wife hurried after him, a papoose in her arms, a small child at her skirts. We didn't often see Indians in town and I was fascinated by the buckskins and beads." He laughed. "I thought they looked a lot more comfortable than my jacket and trousers. Then one of the women said Ma should send me with them. There were my kind. I had no idea what she meant. It was the first time I realized I was somehow different." The first but not the last time he'd been sharply reminded how people saw him.

He hadn't gotten used to it. Every time he heard a similar comment, his heart shriveled. He'd meant for Charlotte to see how it felt to be always on the outside, but perhaps he should have chosen another story. One that didn't remind him, didn't fill him with dread that Star might experience the same thing.

Charlotte made a sympathetic sound. "How utterly cruel of that woman."

Kody chuckled. "Ma was very angry. I knew it even though she didn't show it. She picked me up and held me on her lap and hugged me tight and

said to the woman, 'Dakota is my son. He's my
kind of boy. He belongs right here.'" Remembering how safe he'd felt in her lap, he swallowed
hard.

Charlotte squeezed his arm. "You ma was right.
You belong right here." She seemed to promise so
much with her simple words.

He let the car creep to the edge of the road and
crawl to a halt.

He let himself look at Charlotte, let himself be
drawn into her gaze, let the warmth in her look
reach deep into his soul where he kept secret
things locked away, where they'd been so long
they were buried in a tangle of webs. It seemed her
look eased open the door and as she talked, the
cobwebs peeled back just a little.

He couldn't turn from Charlotte's gaze. It
offered the same kind of acceptance his ma's arms
had provided. A man could feel safe with her.

He could no longer deny his feelings. He loved
her. Somewhere in the distant recesses of his mind,
he remembered they didn't belong to the same
world. He had no right to even think of loving her,
but right now he wanted to let his thoughts drown
in the warm depths of her eyes.

The pressure of her hand on his arm had a
gentle yet reassuring weight to it. Her touch made
him want to confront people who dared say any-

thing about his heritage. He leaned closer, breathed in her sweet, flowery scent, drank in her welcoming smile. He brushed his knuckles along her chin, enjoying the softness of her skin and the way her gaze clung to his. As if she accepted him just as Ma and Pa did. He wanted to believe it possible.

He kissed her gently, then pulled back and smiled into her eyes. He could live like this, enjoying her presence.

But the reality of who he was could not be avoided. He'd take it with him no matter how far north he rode. He'd live with it every day of his life. He had to accept how it affected his choices. And how it affected everyone he cared about.

"I don't belong anywhere." His voice rasped. "I don't know who I am. I don't know my real mother's name. Or who my father was." His voice dropped to a croak. "Maybe he forced himself on her." He meant to shock Charlotte. But the confession tore his deepest secret, his worst fear from him. "I could be just like him."

Tears glistening in her eyes, she rubbed her hand along his arm. "I think you mean you don't know who your parents are. We all know who *you* are."

Her touch made him want so many things—the chance to be someone, the right to ask for a woman's caress, to marry and have a family. But how could he hope for such things? He didn't belong anywhere. Didn't have anything to offer but an uncertain heritage. "Who am I?"

She smiled. "That's easy. You're a good, kind man with a sense of humor who helps others even when it means a sacrifice."

He ached to believe her. He touched her cheek, her skin as soft as the petals on a wild rose.

And white.

He jerked back. "That's what I do. But who *am* I? I don't belong in the white man's world. I tried living on a reservation and found out I don't belong in the Indian world, either. I am neither. I belong nowhere. Except maybe in Canada."

The warmth of her hand on his arm threatened his determination. "Kody, you can't keep running from who you are. What's more, one of these days you'll discover you have no reason to. You'll realize a man is what's in his heart, and you have a good heart." As if to drive the point home, she pressed her palm to his chest, then red crept up her neck and she drew back, ducking her head.

He wavered, torn between wanting to believe her words and the reality of what he'd seen and heard and lived all his life.

Charlotte sensed his withdrawal and knew it came from years of being conditioned to believe he didn't belong. Even though Martha and Leland loved him and accepted him wholly and freely, in Kody's mind it didn't outweigh what others said and how they'd acted toward him.

She ached to be able to convince him not everyone cared about his heritage. She wished for a way to make him admit those who loved him had more value in his life than those who showed such unkind prejudice. But she knew her words would fall on deaf ears. She could only pray, and she did, fervently, the rest of the way back to Favor.

She'd intended to point out how Star needed him to help her face the comments already coming her way. But Charlotte couldn't contemplate adding to Kody's distress and kept silent on the subject.

They arrived at the Douglas home and Kody parked the car. Charlotte waited outside as he straightened things in the garage. She wanted to say something to bring back the closeness she'd felt in the car before he confessed how he didn't know who he was, but Kody came out carrying his saddle.

"I'm going to take Sam for a ride. He needs the exercise."

Charlotte watched as he cinched the saddle and rode away. This wasn't about Sam needing exercise. This was about Kody dealing with his feelings. *Lord, God, please send healing into his heart. Show him how he is valued by so many people. Help him to see there will always be unkind people. Lord, I love him. Bring him back to me. As always, I submit to Your plan.*

Kody slipped out of the house Sunday morning before anyone stirred. He had almost decided to go to church for the pleasure of seeing Pa enjoy it. But it wasn't Pa he pictured. It was Charlotte. And he could not walk into church for the sole purpose of sitting next to the woman he loved but could not have.

He saddled Sam and rode out of town.

A few minutes later, he passed a very untidy campsite. He stopped to look around, found no one in the vicinity, although the ashes from the fire were still warm.

The general filth reminded him of Shorty and Ratface, but he hadn't seen them in days and figured they'd moved on.

With a shrug of indifference he returned to Sam. "Don't suppose those two are still hanging around, do you?"

Sam snorted.

"Yeah, you're right. A person better be a little cautious just in case."

Sam lifted his head and whinnied.

"You think they're still looking for revenge?"

He jumped into the saddle. "Maybe I won't ride out of town, just in case." He would make sure no one hurt Charlotte.

He reined Sam around and headed back to Favor. "I kind of like having an excuse to hang about."

He could only describe Sam's response as a hearty horse-laugh.

He rose through town, checking the back alleys and hiding places—he knew most of them from childhood games. He saw nothing of the two men. It seemed they had gone elsewhere to conduct their mischief. He headed home. Ma and Pa and Charlotte would soon be back from church. He wasn't any more averse to Ma's cooking than he was to spending the afternoon in Charlotte's company.

Yeah, he knew he played dangerously close to the flames. But he could handle it for a few days. As soon as the shoes for Star came, he would leave. "Won't hurt any to allow myself a little enjoyment," he muttered, and earned a snort from Sam.

Chapter Fourteen

Charlotte was glad for her work at the hospital. Not only did she enjoy it, not only did it make her feel useful and appreciated, it kept her too busy to dwell on her relationship with Kody.

She cherished every minute they spent together and wished it could be more, but Kody left early every morning, working at various ranches earning money. He said he wanted to provide John and Morning with enough supplies for the winter before he rode north.

"I have to check on my pack and see what I still need," he said as they finished supper one day. "Care to help me?"

"As soon as I clean the kitchen."

Martha shooed her away. "I'll do it. You've put

in a long day. Besides, how many nice evenings do we get? Go enjoy."

Charlotte fought a short-lived battle with her conscience. But Martha was right. How many evenings would she get to enjoy Kody's company? Each day she sensed his growing restlessness.

"I need to think of being on the road again soon." He shook his bedroll and hung it over the wooden fence to air.

Charlotte didn't bother to respond. He said it so often she'd begun to think he was trying to convince himself.

"I can't imagine what's taking those people so long to send Star's shoes."

Charlotte leaned against the fence and smiled as she watched him. "It's giving you lots of time to get to know your daughter." They went to the reservation as often as Charlotte could get away. She knew Kody went even more often.

Kody paused from sorting through his things and smiled at her. "Can't complain about that."

"She's one sweet child."

He nodded. "You won't get any argument from me. John and Morning have done well with her."

Charlotte did not miss the flash of pain in his face before he bent over to examine his ax. "She's grown very fond of you. She's going to miss you when you go." She turned and stared across the alley, seeing nothing as pain pinched the back of her heart so cruelly she almost cried out. Star wouldn't be the only one who missed him when he left.

"Still no word from Harry?"

She recognized his intent in asking the question. *You'll be leaving first chance you get, too.* "I showed you his last letter."

It had read: "Glad you found someplace safe. Still looking for a suitable place for us. I'll send for you when I do."

"Huh," said Kody, as if nothing more needed to be said.

But Charlotte's heart burst with things to say. She wanted to beg him to change his mind. But she knew unless something inside him changed, he would be headed to Canada.

As if to confirm her thoughts, he said, "I need to get there in time to find a place before winter. Get some sort of shelter erected, if only a tent of sorts."

She spun around. "You'd live in a tent for the winter? You'll freeze to death."

He leaned back and laughed. "You forget my ancestors have lived in various forms of tents for centuries."

She closed the distance between them and leaned over to give him a hard look. "I don't care how your ancestors lived. All I care about is you."

No. She hadn't blurted out those words. Heat scorched up her cheeks and her eyes watered, but she refused to turn from his surprised look. "Promise me you won't do anything so foolish as to try and survive the winter in a tent." Her words fell to a whisper.

He continued to stare at her, his eyes dark and bottomless, drawing sweetness from her heart. She had said more than she ought, but she meant it and would not take back one word.

She kept her eyes locked on his. She could hear the tick of her heart.

He pushed to his feet. "How can you care for the likes of me?" He sounded doubtful, surprised and pleased at the same time.

She smiled, feeling the sweetness pouring from her heart to her lips. "How can I not?"

He stood motionless. "Don't you know what people will say?"

"Maybe I don't care."

He laughed mockingly. "What would your mother think? Didn't she teach you how you must please people?"

She wanted to refute the suggestion, say it didn't matter. But didn't it? Didn't a person need approval in order to be safe? But approval from whom? Wasn't that the more important question? Surely the opinion of people who loved her and whom she loved should outweigh what others thought.

Kody stepped away. "I need to get this packed up again."

"Wait. You didn't give me a change to answer."

"I think I did."

"It's hard to get over what's been drummed into your head for years."

He snorted. "Ain't that the truth?"

"But, Kody, I am. You pushed me to take the first step toward making a decision on my own. Now look at me. I have a job I get paid for. I am not sitting around waiting to be told what I should do." She realized there was more to it. "I'm not waiting to be told who I am."

He spared her a glance. "That's good." He rolled up his pack and tied it securely. "You're a strong woman. You don't need anyone to tell you anything." He strode into the garage.

She followed. "Why do you let people tell you who you are?"

He kept his back to her and took his time stowing his pack. She stubbornly waited. She wanted an answer.

Finally he faced her, his expression hard. "It doesn't matter what anyone thinks about me. But I won't let anyone I care about be branded so they face the same prejudice."

She jumped out of his way as he strode past her. "If you think you're protecting me…"

But he swung onto Sam's back and rode away.

She slumped against the fence as pain emptied her heart. Had he meant her among those he cared for or only Star? She wanted him to admit he cared, but not like this. Not in such a dismissive way.

She feared he might avoid her after that, but the next evening, he offered to go walking with her. They wandered back to the park where he'd kissed her. She wondered if he took her there for that reason, but they only walked through without stopping at the bench, even though she'd slowed her steps, giving him plenty of opportunity to do so.

The next evening, the wind blew ferociously and they stayed indoors playing checkers. Charlotte wasn't good at planning her moves. So she played recklessly, carelessly, eliciting hoots of laughter from Kody as he captured her kings as fast as she earned them.

The following evening burned so hot they sat in the shade of the house and listened to the sounds of summer. Martha and Leland sat beside them. Leland said, "I have agreed to take the pulpit the first of the month."

"Good for you, Pa."

"I want you to be there."

Charlotte saw the way Kody's muscles tightened even though he didn't move.

"Could you not do this one thing for your Pa?" Leland begged.

"I'll see."

After Martha and Leland went inside, Charlotte sat quietly at Kody's side. She sensed his struggle. She knew he wanted to please his pa, yet he had his own internal battles to fight. Wanting him to know she cared, she reached for his hand.

He stiffened and she expected him to pull away. Instead, he turned his hand so their palms rested against each other and their fingers twined. "Whatever I decide, someone is going to be hurt."

"Your pa will be hurt if you don't go. This is important to him."

"I know how people will react to me being there."

"I should hope most of them would rejoice. After all, isn't church supposed to be a place of healing?"

He snorted.

Suddenly, something she'd struggled with the past several days seemed so clear. "I've been trying to understand an important truth. I think it's more important to listen to what people who care about us think than to give weight to what people who don't care about us might say. But what's even more important is what we think about ourselves as people God created."

He considered her words. "I'm glad you've come to that conclusion. It seems like a good one for you."

She wanted to point out it might well apply to him, but he squeezed her hand gently, sending her a silent warning to let it go, and she knew now was not the time. She would continue to pray for God to teach him the same truth in His way.

Charlotte was weeding the garden a few days later when Kody rode into the yard. He barely let Sam stop before he leaped from the saddle and rushed to her side. "They've come." He waved a parcel, then glanced toward the house and lowered both his voice and the parcel. "I don't want Ma and Pa to know about this. It would make them wonder." He nodded toward the garage.

She pulled off her gloves as she joined him inside. "Open it. Let's see how they look."

He had the package half-open before she finished. From the box he lifted a pair of white boots fixed together with a metal bar. "How's she supposed to walk in these?"

Charlotte pulled a sheet of paper from the box. "Here's instructions." She glanced through them.

"It says she's to wear them day and night and there are directions of how to adjust the bar to turn her foot a little more each day."

He tossed the shoes back in the box. "They look like instruments of torture. How can I do this to Star?"

'There's a handwritten note on the bottom that says her clubfoot is only moderate and should respond well to correction."

"I guess I have to try it. She deserves a chance to see if this will help." He put everything back in the box and hid it behind his saddle. "I'll go out tomorrow." He faced her. "Are you working tomorrow?"

She shook her head. He already knew she had the day off.

"Will you come with me?"

"I'd love to." She enjoyed visiting John and Morning and loved Star's bright spirit. But the biggest reason for going was to spend more time with Kody. Maybe tomorrow would be the day he let go of his hurts from the past and became willing to face a future with her. She dreamed and prayed he would come to that decision. Now that the shoes were here, he would be leaving any day. The idea he might leave without changing his mind… She took a deep breath to stop the way her insides threatened to wither. She considered her options. She could pack up and go with him. She gladly would endure the hardships of the North. But unless he stopped running from who he was, he would not take her along. He would never consider making her his wife. *Please, God, show him Your great love. Let him see it's enough.*

She got up early the next morning and took special pains with her hair. She'd been wearing it in a bun since she started work at the hospital, but today she left it down and held back from her face with pretty little combs. She chose her nicest cotton dress—nothing fancy about it, but the blue fabric brought out the color in her eyes. She needed nothing to bring out the color in her cheeks. That came from anticipation.

Both she and Kody hurried through breakfast. As they went outside, Kody said, "I suppose she'll need some stockings to wear inside them."

"I saw some at Boulter's."

"Let's go get them." He checked the time. "It's early. Let's walk."

Several people were at the store when they arrived. Charlotte waved at Amy and hurried toward the display of children's clothing.

Amy left her father serving a man and wife to assist Charlotte and Kody.

The woman at the counter turned to stare rudely

and spoke loudly enough for all to hear. "We aren't the only ones with things gone missing. Seems to have started about the time he rode back into town."

Charlotte stared at the woman. She heard a rumble of comments and shifted her gaze around the room. Most people refused to meet her look. Mr. Boulter, however, didn't mind sending her a very pointed look.

She felt Kody stiffen, didn't need to look at him to know he'd heard.

Amy touched his arm. "Don't pay them any attention. Some people have nothing better to do than gossip and speculate. Now, how can I help you?"

Charlotte stole a glance at Kody, not surprised he kept his face as expressionless as a wooden mask. But she knew beneath his indifferent demeanor lay hurt.

"Thank you, Amy." She appreciated the girl's defense of Kody. "Are those what you want?" She pointed to the stockings and waited for Kody to decide.

"Fine." He followed Amy to the register, Charlotte on his heels. Glowering, the outspoken woman stepped back as if afraid he'd get too close.

"I have cash." Kody's low, measured tones were meant for everyone to hear as they strained forward to see what he would do.

Amy wrapped the stockings carefully in pretty tissue paper as if to show her father and everyone else she didn't agree with their censure, and then she grabbed some candy. "My gift."

"Thanks." Kody nodded and marched for the door, his stride long but his steps unhurried.

Charlotte paused at the doorway. She wanted to say something, but what could she say that wouldn't make this worse? She was no good at defying people like Amy did. But she gave the woman and Mr. Boulter a hard, accusing look before she followed Kody.

It took them far less time to make it back to the house than it had taken to get to the store. Charlotte gasped to catch her breath as they stepped into the yard. They wasted no time climbing into the car and driving away.

Not until the town was behind them did either of them speak.

"Now you know what it's like." Kody sounded as if it hurt to push the words out.

"Like Amy said, some people don't have anything better to do. They're ignorant. Amy was kind, though." She wanted him to acknowledge that not everyone used the same paint in their brush.

"Nothing ever changes."

She smiled. "I beg to differ. Lots of things have changed recently."

He darted her a look, saw her smile and relaxed slightly. "You mean *you've* changed?"

"Does it show?"

He glanced at her again. "I don't think you've changed so much as you finally see who you really are."

"And what is that?"

"Are you begging for compliments?"

"I don't think so." She considered it. "Nope. I just want to hear what you think."

He chuckled.

She didn't care about anything else after she'd brought the sunshine back to his face.

"You are a strong, brave woman who is willing to face challenges."

"You really think so?"

"I know so."

"Then why don't you give me a chance to do it?"

His glance seemed puzzled. "I'm not stopping you."

She wanted him to see that he was. He wouldn't give her a chance to prove she had enough strength to face the kind of remarks she'd heard in the store. "Yes, you are. And the sad thing is, you think you're protecting me."

He stared straight ahead.

She knew he understood her comments and

chose to ignore them. But perhaps he would think about her words. And maybe, God willing, they would make him change.

"Was that the first time you heard things have been stolen around here?" he asked.

"No. Some of the women at the hospital say things have been taken off their clotheslines or from their woodsheds. The matron said things were missing from the storeroom. I can't imagine stealing from a hospital."

"I wonder…"

She waited, and when he didn't seem inclined to finish, she prodded, "What?"

"Well, if I'm not stealing things, then someone else must be."

"Obviously."

He nodded and look thoughtful.

"You think you might know who it is?" she asked.

"I have my suspicions."

"Then tell the sheriff."

"Huh. You think he'd believe me? But there's more than one way to skin a skunk."

"What are you going to do?"

"Catch them. Prove I'm not the one."

She sat back and stared out the window. "What if they're dangerous? You might be hurt."

He grunted. "Not if it's who I think it is."

They arrived at the reservation then, and the

conversation came to an end. She wanted him to promise not to try to stop these men on his own. "Be careful," she murmured before they got out.

Chapter Fifteen

It tickled Kody right down to his toes that Charlotte cared about his safety. He sobered instantly. She made it plain she cared about him in other ways, too. But she had no idea how cruel people could be and he had no desire for her to find out. As soon as he got these shoes on Star, he would head out.

But first, he had to stop whoever was stealing from people around here. Whether or not Ratface and Shorty were the culprits as he suspected, he couldn't be certain Charlotte was safe as long as they hung around. He wouldn't leave until they were locked up or he was certain they'd left the area. He preferred the former over the latter.

He grabbed the box holding the shoes from the backseat and went to greet the Eaglefeathers.

A few minutes later he'd shown the shoes to Morning and John, who looked doubtful. John touched them. "They are very hard."

"Will they not hurt?" Morning asked.

Kody didn't like the idea one bit better than they did. "It's the only way to straighten her foot."

They had stayed a distance from Star as they examined and discussed the shoes, and now they went over and Kody sat on the ground in front of her. "See what I brought you." He let her examine the shoes.

The little girl took her time doing so, then handed them back to him. "No, thank you."

"Star, don't you want to walk and run like the other children?"

"Yes."

"These will straighten your foot so you can."

She searched his eyes, demanding in her unblinking intensity. He wanted to be everything she needed. He wanted her to trust him as her—he faltered—father.

Finally she nodded. "I do as you say."

He helped her put on the new stockings. The shoes weren't easy to put on. She stiffened. Tears filled her eyes as he forced her crooked foot into the boot, but she didn't protest. She fixed him with a hard look that seemed to say, *I'm trusting you to do what is best.*

He hoped and prayed this would work. Finally he got both shoes tied. The bar allowed some movement and he put her on her feet. She couldn't balance and he caught her as she tipped over.

She pushed from his hands and plopped onto her bottom. "I can't walk now." Her voice rang with accusation.

Kody flung a desperate look to Charlotte, saw the glisten of tears in her eyes before she knelt beside Star.

"It takes a long time for your foot to get better." She held out the instruction page. "It says here it's a slow process. It also says you can *learn* to walk in these shoes. Why don't you try again?"

Star gave them each a disbelieving look. Morning and John had backed away but now joined them.

Morning squatted in front of Star. "You must learn to walk again."

John reached for her hands. "I'll help you."

Star turned her unblinking gaze back to Kody. "You help me."

"I'd like to." Though his inclination was to take those wretched boots and throw them as far as he could. Star had been quite happy hobbling around with her crooked foot. How could she understand this was for her good? He felt he needed to explain it and pulled his daughter onto his lap. "Star, it's not that we don't all love you just the way you are." So bright and keen and sweet, what was not to love? "But if this will fix your foot, well, I think you should try it. Don't you?"

She nodded. "I will walk."

He held her hands and helped her to her feet. His heart twisted as she grimaced and her face paled. She struggled a few yards.

"I not walk." She yanked away from him and dropped to her hands and knees. "I not want to walk anymore."

John scooped up the child and pressed her to his chest.

Kody closed his eyes as Star buried her face against John's shoulder. He didn't want to do this any more than Star did. But didn't she deserve a chance?

Charlotte touched his arm. "Give her time to get used to them."

He reached for her hand and held it, willingly accepting her sympathy and understanding.

"We'll give it a fair try. Is everyone agreed?" he asked.

John and Morning nodded, though their eyes filled with distress.

Charlotte squeezed Kody's hand. He knew she understood how much it hurt to have to do this and he clung to her strength.

Morning prepared lunch, but Kody had no appetite. He couldn't bear to watch Star crawl about on her hands and knees, her face drawn with pain and determination.

He put aside his plate and sat on the ground beside her. "Sometimes people have to hurt you because they love you." He didn't expect that made any more sense to her than it did to him. "I only want to see your foot better. That's what we all want."

The other three murmured agreement.

He remembered the candy Amy had given him and pulled it from his pocket. He handed it to Star.

"Thank you," she said, but stared at it with little interest. Finally, she popped it into her mouth all the while staring into Kody's face with an accusing look. "Good," she murmured without enthusiasm.

His heart ached clear to his toes.

They didn't stay long after that. It was too difficult watching Star struggle.

"You will see that she wears them?" Kody asked John as he walked with them to the car.

"Yes. It is the only way to fix her foot." The resignation in his friend's voice echoed Kody's own feelings.

He slipped out after supper while Charlotte helped clean up, hoping to ride away before she discovered his purpose. But as he tossed the saddle onto Sam's back, he heard the door shut and knew he wouldn't succeed.

"Oh. You're going somewhere."

He ducked his head to hide his smile at how disappointed she sounded. Could be she had come to enjoy their evening hours together as much as he did. His smile fled. He walked in dangerous territory, allowing himself this forbidden pleasure— loving her, but knowing he had to ride away. "I've got something to tend to."

She came around Sam so she could see him. "You're going to try and catch whoever is stealing things around here, aren't you?"

"Huh."

She grabbed his arm, forcing him to face her. "Tell me you aren't going alone."

Her concern was honey to his soul. Oh, to have this interest in his welfare for the rest of his life. He sucked in the smell of horseflesh and forced resolve into his thoughts. "Matter of fact, Jed Hawkes is going with me. I figured no one would believe me if *I* turned in two scoundrels."

"Two? You're going after two?" She sucked in air and seemed to struggle to control her reaction. "Jed's a good man. I know him and Bess from church, but two evil men? Won't you need more help than that?"

He touched her cheek, wanting to ease her

worry. "This pair won't be more than the two of us can handle."

Her expression relaxed as he rubbed his knuckles against her kitten-soft skin. Then she grabbed his hand and squeezed it between hers. "How can you be so sure?"

He couldn't stand her distress. "I think it's Shorty and Ratface. We both know they're half-ways cowards."

"You think they're still around here? That campsite on the way to the reservation has long been abandoned."

"I saw another campsite that looked like it had exploded. Guessed it was probably them." He reluctantly extricated his hand so he could tighten the cinch.

She touched his shoulder. "Kody, be careful."

Her words held more power than a loaded gun, and he straightened and faced her, knowing it was probably the most dangerous thing he'd ever done in his life. "Charlotte, I ain't no fool. I don't take chances."

She nodded, but her eyes remained troubled.

He leaned over and kissed her gently, long-ingly. If only… But there could be no *if only*s. He let his lips linger a heartbeat, excusing himself, saying he had to reassure her, but promising it would be the last time he kissed her. Soon as he completed tonight's task, he would have no further excuse for staying.

He'd been right. The campsite belonged to Shorty and Ratface. And the pair was there. Kody and Jed stayed out of sight, watching them. Then followed as the the scoundrels set out at dusk. Shorty and Ratface made no attempt to be quiet, nor did they check the trail to see if anyone followed.

"Like I told Charlotte, they aren't the reddest apples on the tree," Kody murmured. But smart or not, if these two were guilty of what he suspected, they had to be stopped, and he didn't suppose they would take kindly to someone putting an end to their free pickin's. Cowards could be deadly when cornered. He knew enough to be careful.

They followed the pair to town, then down a back alley to a darkened house.

"The Sloans," Jed whispered. "It's no secret they've gone to visit their daughter in Missoula."

Jed and Kody hung back, watching, as the other two prowled around the house, gunny sacks draped over their shoulders. They waited as Shorty tried the back door, found it wasn't locked and tossed aside his crowbar. When the two scuttled inside, Jed and Kody dropped silently from their mounts and eased up to the yawning door. When the pair returned with their arms full, Kody and Jed greeted them with drawn guns.

"Put that stuff down real slow and get your hands in the air."

"I'll hold them. You go get the sheriff," Jed said.

Kody nodded. Any other way and suspicion would be cast on him.

He returned in a few minutes with the sheriff and sighed with satisfaction as the pair were cuffed and dragged off to jail.

The sheriff leaned back in his chair as Kody and Jed gave their statements. "I thank you for your help." He fixed Kody with an appraising look. "The town could use more men like you."

Kody shook hands with the lawman and strode out. It felt good to hear such words. He wished he could stay, put down roots here, marry a certain young woman and be a father to his daughter, but in the end, nothing had changed. He was still a half-breed. He still had no idea who he was or what he'd come from. Nor would the sheriff's approval change the way Mr. Boulter treated him. He did not intend to share the realities of his life with Charlotte or Star. It wouldn't be fair to either of them. He'd let Charlotte know Ratface and Shorty wouldn't be bothering her. And then…

He pulled his hat down over his eyes. He'd about run out of excuses for not leaving.

* * *

Pa was to preach this morning. Kody planned to go to church and hear him. He didn't have a whole lot of choice, seeing as he'd hung around long after he should have gone, telling himself he had to see Pa well enough to take over his regular tasks before he left.

He'd intended to spend less time with Charlotte, knowing he might as well get used to living without her company. Instead, he spent every possible moment with her. Evenings after they both finished work for the day were gentle, satisfying hours he knew he would relive over and over when he settled in Canada, but her days off were…

He closed his eyes at the bittersweetness of them.

They usually went to the reservation. It provided a handy excuse for spending the day with her. But seeing Star grow more and more frustrated with those torturous shoes was like a lance straight through his heart. The cheerful, outgoing, sweet child grew unhappy and discontent. Her eyes filled with dark accusation when he visited. Not even the toys he took erased it. He hated being the cause of her pain. He wanted nothing more than to take those shoes off and burn them. Only the hope she might one day walk properly gave him the strength to endure her misery.

Charlotte understood his pain, perhaps even shared it, for she, too, loved Star. He found comfort in her presence, in the way she touched his arm. And yes, despite his vow otherwise, he kissed her again. Almost every time they left the reservation. He needed to feel her love and accept it for a few minutes. The memory of those kisses and her sweet love would have to last him a long, long time. He would finish packing today. He would leave first thing tomorrow morning.

He stood in the middle of his bedroom, holding several western novels, trying to decide which ones to pack for reading material and which to leave behind. If he wasn't such a sentimental fool he would simply buy new ones, but he wanted the memories associated with these familiar ones. He randomly selected the one in his right hand and dropped it on the bed, along with the picture of him taken with his parents when he started school and the Bible presented to him for perfect attendance in Sunday school. He snorted. Wasn't hard to be there every Sunday when your father was the preacher. He would probably never read it, but again, sentimental value made him decide to take it.

He looked around the room. What else did he want to take? Nothing. He meant to start over.

Groaning, he sank to the edge of his bed.

He didn't want to leave.

But he'd run out of excuses to stay.

He had to go. The sooner, the better. His feet like lead on every step, he made his way downstairs for breakfast.

They drove to church, so Pa wouldn't be worn-out by the time they arrived. Kody hung back as they stepped into the churchyard. "Best if I wait a bit and sit in the back."

Ma and Pa paused, exchanged a look and Ma turned to argue.

"Go ahead. Everyone will want to greet Pa."

Reluctantly they left him. Charlotte stayed beside Kody and slipped her hand through the crook of his arm. He squeezed his elbow to his side, pressing her hard to him, and fought an urge to declare his undying love. He noted many surprised glances in his direction. They convinced him to keep his mouth shut on the matter. Charlotte deserved acceptance, not the kind of looks several of the women sent his way. Then Jed saw him and waved. He and Bess hurried to join them.

"Glad to see you," Jed said. "I hoped you'd be here. I have a favor to ask."

"I'll do whatever I can. What is it?"

"I'm rounding up some horses tomorrow. They've been running free all year. I could sure use help from a man like you."

Kody kept his face expressionless, but Jed's words raced through him with a force sucking at his lungs. *A man like you.* Jed meant it as a good thing. "I'll be there first light." Another delay. And how he welcomed it.

They hurried inside. Jed and Bess indicated they should sit in the same pew and Kody gratefully accepted, sliding in beside Charlotte.

The congregation stood to sing the first hymn. He didn't bother opening the hymnal but sang words as familiar as Pa's face. Charlotte's clear, sweet voice joined his. A deep joy filled his heart. This felt as good as coming home.

And then Pa took his place at the pulpit, and Kody strained toward his words. Pa's speech was still slightly slurred. He spoke slower than he once had and he paused often as he struggled to find a word, but the same familiar power drove the words deep into Kody's heart.

The sermon reminded everyone God's love didn't change. It didn't depend on circumstances, health or what other people said or did. It didn't depend on wealth or belongings. It depended on God's word. His unchanging word.

"We are reminded in Hebrews, chapter thirteen, verse eight, that 'Jesus Christ is the same yesterday, and today and forever.' He has taught us to pray, 'Give us today our daily bread.' My prayer for myself and each of you is we will accept God's promise of love, trust in Him for what we need today and stop fretting about yesterday and tomorrow."

Kody drank in Pa's words like a drought-stricken land would suck in water. He had always believed. He was tired of denying it. *God, You are my God. I have faltered and failed so much. Give me the strength to do as You want, and the wisdom to know what it is.*

He squeezed Charlotte's hand briefly, wanting to share his feelings with her. She smiled, and he knew from the glistening in her eyes she understood this moment was special.

Chapter Sixteen

Charlotte rushed home with her exciting news, hoping Kody would be back from helping Jed Hawkes. She laughed out of sheer joy. Yesterday had been more than she dreamed possible in her prayers. She'd sensed Kody's doubts disappearing as his father preached, been aware of the change in him even before he turned to her and smiled. She rejoiced when he'd gone to his father after the sermon. They'd spoken quietly, then Leland hugged Kody. Even from where she stood, Charlotte had seen the glisten of tears in Leland's eyes. Her own vision blurred as Martha joined them, and Kody hugged her. She'd prayed for Kody's healing and it thrilled her to be able to watch it.

And now news like she'd never expected. God

certainly knew how to answer above and beyond her wildest dreams.

She went in the back gate and almost cheered when she saw Kody coming from the corral. She hurried to his side. "I have the best news!"

He quirked an eyebrow. "I can't even begin to guess what it might be."

"You wouldn't in a hundred years!"

"Then maybe you should just tell me."

She grabbed his hand. "Matron told us today a special doctor is coming to visit."

"Uh-huh."

"He can fix bones."

Kody again quirked an eyebrow. He obviously wasn't getting how great an opportunity this could be.

She slowed down and spelled it out carefully. "Matron told us how he's fixed broken arms that weren't set correctly, how he's helped people with something wrong with their hips and—" she squeezed his hand hard "—he's had very good success with fixing clubfeet. He could fix Star."

Kody jerked back, pulling his hand from her grasp. "Are you joking?"

"No." Why wasn't he excited about this possibility?

"Then let me point out a few facts. For starters she's an Indian and won't be allowed to see the doctor. Besides, the doctor told John her foot couldn't be fixed."

"This doctor *is* fixing them."

He stared at her like he'd never seen her before. "White children, maybe."

"A clubfoot is the same whatever the color of your skin."

"Except the color of your skin makes people treat you differently."

She jutted out her chin. "Not everyone. Do I treat you differently? Do your parents? Bess and Jed? And probably hundreds of others if you care to pay attention."

"You expect Star to understand that?"

She couldn't believe his resistance. "Kody, she deserves a chance. You know those shoes aren't working."

He took off the saddle and pushed past her to carry it to the garage.

She followed. He had to see that Star needed this. "Couldn't you at least take her to this doctor and get his opinion?"

He draped his saddle over the stand before he answered. "I have no intention of giving people a chance to tell me to take her back to the reservation where she belongs."

Anger erupted from Charlotte's brain, erasing caution, fueling her words with fire. "Kody Douglas, you know something? This isn't about Star and her facing negative comments—"

"Prejudice."

"I don't care what you call it, because I realize something. This isn't about her. This is about you. You don't want to face those unkind, untrue remarks. You'd sooner run. How far do you think you'll have to run to outrun yourself? Canada won't be far enough. Alaska wouldn't be. Isn't it time you stopped running and faced life? Your life?" She stomped away, not caring if she'd offended him. Partway out the door, she paused. "You know, Kody, I almost thought I loved you." Her anger shifted so suddenly to pain she cried out. She loved him whether or not he would ever accept it.

She ran to her room and threw herself on her bed.

He talked about being strong, expecting her to be so, yet he ran from his own problems.

She breathed slowly, calming her anger, letting her pain dissipate. Then she turned to prayer. *God, I know You've sent this doctor. Please make Kody see how it could be the best thing for Star. She deserves this chance. Please, let Kody love me as I love him.*

She remained there for a few minutes, then hurried downstairs determined to find a way to convince Kody to change his mind.

The look he gave her as he sat down to supper warned her he would hear nothing more on the subject. She ducked her head. She would find a way to say more.

However, he made it impossible to talk to him that night. He played checkers with Leland, then held a skein of yarn as Martha rolled it into a ball.

Charlotte sent him pleading looks and sighed heavily.

Martha looked up. "Is there something wrong, dear?"

"No, I'm fine." She crossed to the window. "It looks so lovely out. It'd be nice to go for a walk."

"Go right ahead," Martha said kindly, unaware of the tension between Charlotte and Kody. "I'm almost done here. Kody, why don't you go with her?"

Kody yawned loudly. "I'm tired, Ma. I think I'll go to bed early."

"Another time, then?" Charlotte knew he understood the warning in her voice, but he only gave her a dark look that said he would not give her another chance to mention this subject.

She sent him an equally hard look, silently informing him she wasn't prepared to give up. She didn't know how she'd convince him, but she would do so if humanly possible.

But next morning she still hadn't come up with

a way to do so, let alone how to get the chance. He wasn't at breakfast. Her heart stopped working when she saw his empty place. Had he gone to Canada without saying goodbye?

"Gone back to the Hawkes'," Martha said. "Says he promised to break some horses for Jed."

Charlotte thanked God she would get another chance.

Kody sat at the table when she returned from the hospital that afternoon.

"We must talk," she murmured.

"Nothing left to say."

"I think there is."

He simply shook his head.

Martha hurried in from the front room. "There's a letter for you." She handed it to Charlotte.

Charlotte recognized Harry's writing and opened the envelope, pulled out the sheet of paper and unfolded it. She read the message twice, wondering that she felt nothing.

"Let me guess," Kody's voice rasped. "He still doesn't have any room for you."

"Listen to what he says. 'We've found a house finally. I've enclosed a money order for a ticket for you to join us. We've missed you. The children ask after you constantly.'" She shook the envelope and a money order fell out.

"You'll be leaving, then?"

She stared at the letter she'd been waiting for since she'd been abandoned.

"I miss the children." She could go and help Nellie, make herself indispensable, as Mother had advised. Certainly Nellie would appreciate her now. "Listen to the rest. He signs himself, 'Lovingly, Harry,' and 'P.S. Nellie is expecting another baby.'" She slowly folded the page and returned it to the envelope, along with the money order.

She waited for Kody to say something, anything to convince her she shouldn't go, but he stared into his cup of tea as if he hoped to discover all the secrets of the world there.

"Kody, can you give me one reason I shouldn't buy a ticket and leave?" She loved him. Guessed he must know it by now. But her love meant nothing unless he returned it.

Slowly, he brought his head up and stared at her, his eyes dark, revealing nothing. Nothing at all. Finally he shook his head. "You should go to Harry. It's what you wanted from the start. It's where you belong."

Her insides tensed. She gathered up every ounce of her courage. "I could belong anywhere I'm wanted."

"He's family. Where else should you be?"

His words swept clean her heart, cleansing it of

hope, leaving her empty and hurting. She pushed back from the table and fled to her room, where she stared out the window. She tried to pray, but her empty heart yielded no words.

"Supper," Martha called up the stairs, and Charlotte forced resolve into her heart. She could face this. Wasn't Kody always telling her she was strong?

Her head high, she marched into the kitchen and took her place, thankful Leland was full of talk about a visit he'd had with the church elders, arranging for him to resume his role as pastor.

The meal over, Charlotte rose to clear the table.

"Ma, Pa."

The sound of something both hard and reluctant in Kody's voice stopped her in her tracks.

"I'll be leaving tomorrow morning."

"Leaving?" Martha sounded surprised.

"For Canada."

"But I thought…" Leland grabbed Kody's arm. "After…" He struggled to get his words out. "Sunday. I thought you would be staying." Leland sent Martha a pleading look.

Martha nodded and voiced the words Leland couldn't pull from his shocked mind. "We both thought you had accepted who you are, who God made you to be."

"I can't deny my faith. But my reality is still the same. I don't fit."

Charlotte gripped the plate she held so hard her fingers cramped. She wanted to grab him, shake him hard until he admitted he was accepted by some, not by others. But what mattered most was what he thought of himself.

"Kody, my son—" Martha's voice rang with pain "—when will you ever forgive those who have been cruel to you?"

He pushed from the table. "Ma, I can forgive them all I want, but it won't change them. I can handle what they say about me, but—" he shot Charlotte a look so full of pain she almost cried out in protest "—I won't let others be branded the same way. This is goodbye. I'll be gone before anyone is up tomorrow."

"No," Charlotte called, but he slipped out the door before she could say anything to change his mind. She wanted to say she didn't care what people said. She loved him enough to ignore it. People who mattered knew he was a good man.

Martha took Leland into the front room. They spoke quietly, but Charlotte didn't need to hear their words to know they sought ways to deal with Kody's impending departure.

As she washed dishes, she sought her own way. Found nothing to ease the twisting of her insides. She didn't cry, her pain beyond tears. Somehow she had to go on from here. She could only do it with God's help. She remembered Leland's sermon. She had only to trust God one day at a time.

Charlotte lay in bed. Kody had ridden away yesterday morning as she'd watched from her bedroom window. He'd glanced back, seen her there, gave the barest tilt of his head, then kicked Sam into a gallop.

She moaned. The house shuddered. She smiled crookedly. Even the house missed him. She bolted upright. The house rattled. She raced to the window. The air looked gray as shameful laundry. The northern horizon rolled with a gigantic black cloud.

Kody was out there somewhere. She prayed he'd found shelter.

She tried to block out the sound of the wind as she prepared for work.

It blew all day, through the night and all the next day. Charlotte thought of the Eaglefeathers and prayed they would be okay. She thought of the people living in the drought-stricken area and prayed for their safety. She tried not to remember stories of people lost in such a storm. How their bodies had been found buried in dirt. She shuddered. What an awful way to die. She wouldn't think Kody could suffer such a fate. He knew enough to find shelter. But what if...? She wouldn't let her thoughts go there and prayed even as she helped clean the hospital.

Next morning people suffering dust pneumonia started to flock to the hospital. The wards were full of coughing. Charlotte raced from patient to patient with water, urging them to drink more. She spoon-fed broth to those too weak to help themselves. She stayed late, knowing how desperately these people needed care.

Long past dark she made her weary way home. Martha had left a plate of food in the oven for her. She tried to eat it, but hardly had the energy to lift the fork to her mouth.

She dragged herself upstairs and sank onto the edge of the bed. Her gaze fell on Harry's letter. He'd asked her to join them. She shook her head. She couldn't leave Matron and the nurses when they needed every pair of hands they could find.

They needed her. It felt good, but it had nothing to do with her need to be needed. This was about doing something of value. She sat straighter. What she did had importance. She considered the idea. For the first time she considered who she was, what she wanted.

She'd been raised to think she must trust Harry to take care of her. She must work to ensure he would, but she didn't need Harry's protection. She'd proved it. She didn't need to kowtow to Nellie in order to have a home. She'd found a perfectly good home here. And even though she couldn't expect to continue to live with Martha and Leland, she could move into the nurses' residence. She had value and purpose. Right here— she pressed her hand to her chest—in her heart, accepting the life God so graciously provided her. *God, thank You for who I am.*

If only she could tell Kody. *Please keep him safe wherever he is.*

Renewed, she quickly penned a note to Harry saying she couldn't leave her job. She put the money order and letter in an envelope and sealed them. She would mail it tomorrow.

Smiling so hard her cheeks hurt, she prepared for bed and fell asleep instantly.

When, next day, she mentioned moving to the nurses' residence, Martha and Leland begged her to board with them. She agreed readily.

Her newfound joy filled her with a bubble of continuous laughter the next few days, marred only by missing Kody and her wish that Star could see the special doctor. Often she gazed to the north, wondering how far Kody had gone. Would he ever stop running? Would he ever come back?

Chapter Seventeen

Kody had every intention of riding hard and fast for Canada when he left Favor, but he had one thing to do first. He rode to the reservation to say goodbye to John and Morning and to give Star one last hug. It took every ounce of his strength to keep from showing any emotion as he held his little daughter. He would never see her again, but he could do one last thing for her. He unlaced those hateful, hurtful boots and tied them to Sam's saddle. "I'll dump them in a ravine somewhere."

He squatted before Star. "You be happy, hear?"

"I don't want you go." She sobbed. "Why you have to?"

"It's for the best." Seems he had to say it so often when it should have been obvious to everyone. "I have to go."

"No, you don't."

He brushed his hand over her hair and stroked her cheek, then pushed to his feet and nodded a last goodbye to Morning and John. But when he returned to the main road he stopped. Somehow, despite his determination to ride fast and far, he couldn't head north. Instead, he turned south, rode a mile, then chose a road to the west. He needed a place far enough from town he could disappear for all intents and purposes. Yet he could be close enough to keep an eye on both Charlotte and Star. And he knew just the place. The Widow Murphy needed a man.

He rode until he reached the Murphy place. Widow Murphy hired him instantly, accepting him without reservation. He chuckled. He like the old lady. Admired her spunk. But it was way past time for her to give up her hard life. He said so every chance he got. She was so crippled she could barely walk. He carried water to the house for her. She moaned as she hobbled to the stove.

"Ma'am, why are you clinging to this ranch? Sell it and move to town, where you can have a few comforts."

"Can't, boy. Who'd I sell it to?"

"Lot of people would be glad of this place." It was a beautiful ranch with lots of grass and water and a big log house her husband had built. "This house is way too big for one woman."

She sighed. "We planned to fill it with kids. Didn't plan for Cyrus to get hisself killed."

"So let someone else fill it with kids. Ain't it time to let it go?"

"Boy, I vowed I would keep this ranch after my good man died. I haven't quit anything in my life. Figure I ain't going to now."

"Sometimes it's okay to change your mind."

"Next you'll be telling me I'm too old to run this place."

He gave her a hard look. "You *are* too old. Stop being so stubborn."

"I ain't old if I don't want to be."

He snorted and stalked from the room. How could she be so blind? She seemed to figure if she chose to believe she wasn't old, she wasn't old. But pretending it wasn't so didn't change the facts.

He faltered on his next step as one thought caught another and twisted together like tangled rope. Widow Murphy ignored the fact of her age. Kody Douglas ignored the fact people cared about him despite his heritage.

He took an uncertain step. He knew Charlotte cared for him. He cared for her. He loved her.

But did she love him enough to face prejudice? Accept his uncertain heritage? Did he want to face it? He knew people could be cruel. Who knew what sort of people the future might bring into his life?

Pa's words blasted through his mind. *Joyfully take what God gives us today. Let Him take care of yesterday and tomorrow.*

Kody's today included a woman he loved and who, he hoped, loved him back.

It included a little girl he wanted to be there for.

He raced back to the house. "I'll be gone a day or two, but I'll be back." He carried in enough water to last Widow Murphy while he was away and filled her wood box to overflowing. "Don't do something stupid while I'm gone, like climb into the loft to see if it needs repair. I'll look after everything when I get back."

He reached Favor at suppertime, turned Sam into the little corral and hurried to the house. He hoped he wasn't too late to stop Charlotte from leaving to join Harry.

He burst through the door.

Three pairs of eyes jerked in his direction. "Ma, Pa, Charlotte. I've come back." He saw only one face—Charlotte's. Something sweet and joyous and completely welcoming flared in her eyes. He couldn't believe how close he'd come to riding away from that.

She set a place at the table for him. Ma and Pa plied him with questions he hoped he answered in a reasonable fashion. He wouldn't be able to think straight until he dealt with two important items.

After supper, he waited until Ma and Pa had left the room before he said to Charlotte, "Did that special doctor come yet?"

"He's coming tomorrow."

"Good. I want to take Star. Will you come with me to the reservation to get her?"

She nodded.

"I'm going to tell her I'm her father."

Charlotte laughed. "Thank God. One prayer answered."

"One?"

She ducked her head. "I have more, but let's deal with this first."

He agreed, even though he wanted to sweep her into his arms and declare his love right there on the spot. But he wanted to do it right. He wanted to allow her to see exactly what he was and have a chance to decide how much it mattered.

Charlotte had the day off, so they left early next morning. He wanted to get Star to the doctor as soon as possible.

It wasn't until he stopped the car at the Eagle-feathers' home that he realized he had no idea what to say. He said as much to Charlotte.

"Seems to me the plain and simple truth is best."

He nodded. He took Morning and John aside first and told them his plan. John squeezed his arm. "It is for the best. We have hoped you would do this."

But Kody feared his confession would upset Star. After all, he intended to turn her world upside down. He grabbed Charlotte's hand as he went to face his daughter.

Charlotte squeezed reassuringly. "I'll pray," she whispered.

He had her support and God's help. He could do this.

He sat cross-legged in front of Star, liking how she looked in the dress Charlotte had made her, seeing her light eyes, knowing they set her apart, yet her eyes were beautiful. He would teach her to be proud of how she looked and her heritage. Just as Ma and Pa had taught him. It had taken a while for it to get through his stubborn resistance, but it finally had. He took a deep breath, glad when Charlotte stood close by, offering encouragement yet understanding he and Star had to deal with this alone.

"Star, I have something important to tell you."

She squinted at him. "No more boots."

He laughed. "This isn't about your foot. It's about who you are."

"I am Star."

His bright, shining child. He wanted to hug her close, but needed to face her to make this announcement, needed to give her room to react however she chose. "Star, you have light eyes because your mommy had light eyes."

She stared at him.

"Her name was Winnoa and she died when you were a baby. That's why I left you with Morning and John."

She didn't blink. Her intense gaze made his eyes sting.

"I am your father."

Her eyes widened. She looked to John and Morning. "They are my momma and poppa."

"They both love you very much and will always love you. But I am your father."

"Why you leave me?"

All his arguments became dust before her accusations. "I thought it best."

"Not best."

"I know that now. I want to take care of you. I want you and I to be together."

She nodded. "Like a real father?"

"Yes. Like a real father."

Her smile rivaled the sun for brightness. "I like that." She shifted her gaze back to Morning and John. "I not want to leave my momma and poppa."

"You won't have to until you're ready." He

didn't have a place for her yet. There were so many things to work out.

Star scrambled to her feet and threw her arms around his neck. "My real own daddy."

Behind him, Charlotte sniffed.

He laughed and hugged his little daughter. "I love you, Star Douglas."

She hugged her arms around his neck so tight he almost choked, but he didn't mind. Not in the least.

She leaned back against his arms. "I know'd you was my father."

"You did? Who told you?"

"Nobody. I know'd 'cause you made me wear bad boots. Only a father would make a little girl do it."

He crushed her to his chest. "It is because I love you."

Her warm little arms stole around his neck and she pressed her face to his cheek. "Me, too."

Charlotte, eyes gleaming, knelt at his side and patted Star's back.

After a few minutes he shifted Star so he could look into her face. "Because I love you, I have one more thing I want you to do."

She nodded slowly, her eyes so full of trust it hurt his heart.

"I want to take you to see a special doctor who might be able to fix your foot."

"Will it hurt?"

"I can't say. You'll have to ask the doctor."

She nodded. "Okay."

Kody didn't want to rush away, but Morning and John encouraged him to get her to the doctor.

Charlotte led them down the hall of the hospital to the waiting room.

A nurse rose from behind a wooden desk. "Why have you brought that child in here?"

"Nurse Sampson—" Charlotte began.

Many grown men quaked at the way she spoke. He was finished with quaking and running and for Star he would face someone ten times Nurse Sampson's size and noise. "My daughter needs to see the doctor."

Behind him he heard words like *dirty Indian*. But one woman, who stood to his right, mumbled, "Poor thing."

The nurse jerked her head back and seemed to get six inches taller. "Indians are not welcome here." She shooed at them.

"I will see the doctor," Kody insisted.

"Ain't that why he's here?" the woman to his right demanded.

Several others added their vocal support. The nurse sat down. "Very well. You can stay, but I can't promise the doctor will see you." She sniffed.

The doctor not only saw her, he said, "This is a fairly simple thing. I think it can be fixed."

Star give him one of her intense looks. "You can make me so I can walk right?"

The doctor leaned over until eye level with Star. "I think so."

"It hurt?"

"You'll have to wear a cast for a while. You'll be stiff and sore as you learn to walk again, but it won't be much for a brave girl like you. Not for someone who has walked on this crooked foot for four years."

"Not like bad boots?" she demanded.

Kody explained about the special shoes. The doctor assured Star it wouldn't be like that at all.

Star nodded soberly. "I want to walk right."

"Then let's do it."

Kody signed papers and discussed payment. His Canada fund, no longer needed for that purpose, would do.

Then he and Charlotte took Star to meet her grandpa and grandma.

Ma and Pa were thrilled to know they had a granddaughter. Kody understood he'd robbed them of four precious years, but they would never point it out. They would take what they had now and enjoy it. As Pa said, enjoying what the present offered.

Star hung back shyly for about two minutes, then started in on a long story about her doll. Ma and Pa couldn't keep their eyes off her.

"Can I leave her with you while Charlotte and I go for a walk?" Kody asked.

No one protested.

Charlotte let him take her hand as they walked down the street. He didn't speak and she waited, knowing this walk had a purpose. She'd seen a difference in Kody from the moment he rode back to town. His eyes were clearer, his face had lost those hard lines. She rejoiced that Star would get her foot straightened and Kody was prepared to be Star's father, but she hoped his return had another purpose. One including her.

He led her past the church and through the little gate into the cemetery. They passed several monuments. Kody stopped before a small marker under a big elm tree. He pulled her close to his side. "My mother's grave."

She read the inscription: *Mother of Dakoka Charles Douglas*. A long, bony finger of shock scratched up her spine. She'd known Kody didn't know his mother's name, but to look at cold, hard proof made it real in a way she hadn't accepted until now.

"I'm sorry," she whispered.

"For what?"

So many things. The fact he didn't know his mother's name or who his father was. That it seemed to matter so much to him.

"I thought I'd learn to live with it, but instead, I've been running from it, as you pointed out."

"I had no right." She'd never intended to hurt him.

"I'm glad you did. I thought I could pretend it didn't matter if I kept running from who I am. But I don't want to run anymore. I want to stay right here and raise Star." He turned and put his arms around her—his strong, loving arms.

She looked up, letting everything she felt fill her smile.

He drank it in as he studied her eyes, ran his gaze down her cheek, settled on her mouth. She waited for him to confess his love and kiss her.

Instead, he eased back fractionally. It felt like he'd moved ten feet. Cold lumped in the bottom of her stomach. He'd said nothing about including her in his change of plans.

He glanced toward the grave marker. "You see my past—uncertain in so many ways. I can't promise people won't judge you poorly because of me. But I love you, and if you'll have me I can promise to love you as long as I live."

Her insides sang with joy. "Kody Douglas, I

love you. I can't change my past. I can't guarantee anything about the future except my undying love. But today is ours. Let's take God's good gifts and enjoy them."

"I would like to share today and whatever the future holds with you and Star and any children—"

She laughed. "One step at a time."

"One day at a time." He kissed her then. Gently, sweetly, a kiss full of love and promise and joy.

Epilogue

Four months later

The October day was perfect. Shimmering yellow leaves danced on the poplar trees. The air glowed in the golden light peculiar to autumn.

Charlotte breathed in deeply, inhaling the rich scent of the season. She wanted to hold the smells, devour the sights, cherish each feeling so she would never forget one detail of this, her wedding day.

She'd chosen a pale pink taffeta for the simple tailored dress Martha helped her make. It would serve her for special occasions for years to come. Her bouquet was a generous spray of tiny sunflowers from Nurse Chester's garden.

"Is it time?" Star demanded, pulling Charlotte's

attention back to the small room where they waited for the ceremony to begin.

"Any minute now." Her words were soft, confident. Over the past few months she and Kody had grown in their love for and understanding of each other. She'd thrilled to see how he started to walk down the sidewalks with the confidence of a man who belonged. His growing faith challenged her own spiritual growth. How she enjoyed praying together with him, sharing her doubts, her triumphs and the ordinary events of her day. She loved having him share his life with her.

She felt the smile fill her eyes with joy, felt it wrap around her heart with assurance at the depth of her love for Kody, of his for her.

"Do I look pretty?" Star's voice reminded Charlotte of the presence of others.

Star wore a rose-pink dress. Her cast had come off two weeks ago. She could barely contain her pleasure and pride at being able to walk with a barely noticeable limp. Charlotte leaned over and hugged her. "You are beautiful. I hope your daddy can stop staring at you long enough to notice me."

Star giggled, then turned serious. "Now you'll be my momma?"

"Indeed I will and I'm so happy about it." She hugged the child. Star whispered, "Momma," in her ear. Charlotte wondered if her heart could hold any more joy.

She turned to Emma, her bridesmaid. "You'll be stealing hearts left and right yourself." Emma had joined the hospital staff during the summer, and she and Charlotte had soon become fast friends. Emma, practical to the core, seldom bothered to dress up. She wore a uniform for work and simple cotton dresses for church. She usually kept her thick blond hair in a tight bun, as suited a nurse, she insisted when Charlotte tried to talk her into letting it hang loose. But Emma had allowed Charlotte to have her way for the wedding and her hair hung in shimmering waves halfway down her back.

The pianist played the processional and Star headed down the aisle.

Emma grinned at Charlotte. "You are positively glowing. I hope you don't ignite before you get properly hitched." She kissed Charlotte on the cheek and hugged her, then followed Star. She'd refused to do the prissy half-step considered appropriate for weddings.

Charlotte smiled as her friend swung down the aisle with the boldness and assurance of the strong woman she was. Charlotte took a deep breath to still her demanding heart, which urged her to run to Kody's arms. She stepped to the doorway. Harry

had been unable to come, saying Nellie needed
him in the last stages of confinement, so Charlotte
had asked Jed to accompany her down the aisle.
She and Kody had become good friends with Jed
and Bess. Clinging to Jed's arm, she stepped into
the sanctuary. The church was full. John and
Morning sat by Kody's parents. She didn't take
time to identify any of the others but shifted her
gaze to the front.

Her lungs refused to work when she saw
Kody standing at the front, resplendent in a
black suit his father had persuaded him to wear.
He'd recently cut his hair and he looked very
debonair. He could pass for a successful busi-
nessman. In the last few months he had continued to work for Widow Murphy. Star had
divided her time between the Eaglefeathers and
her new grandma and grandpa. In a few days,
she would join Kody and Charlotte at the
Murphy ranch.

"It suits me," Kody often said of the ranch.
"Wild and free. Besides, what would Mrs. Murphy
do without me?"

He smiled from the front of the church, and
Charlotte's lungs remembered to work. She held
his gaze as she made her way up the aisle. She
heard the whispers and aahs as she passed those in
attendance, but she had eyes for no one but Kody.

She reached his side, took his hand and let her breath ease out.

As in a dream, she repeated her vows. Not until Leland told Kody he could kiss his bride and Kody's lips met hers in a vow of eternal love, did she feel like the dream ended. Or had it just begun?

Martha, with the help of the church ladies, had prepared a tea for afterward. Kody seemed perfectly at home with everyone. She could hardly believe how distant he'd kept himself not so long ago.

And then the tea things were cleared away and gifts piled in front of them. Together they opened them—towels, fancy dishes, sheets and other essentials.

Later, dusk settled like a pale gray cloak as they climbed into the black truck Kody had purchased, insisting they needed better transportation than horses to take them back and forth to the Murphy ranch.

Someone had left a light burning in the living room of the ranch house, and it beamed a golden welcome as they drove into the yard.

Kody leaned over and kissed Charlotte thoroughly before he jumped from the truck and hurried around to help her out. She looked around, expecting to be led to the small house Mrs.

Murphy provided her hired man, but Kody led her up the path toward the big house.

"What…?" Then she realized Mrs. Murphy must have given them access to the house for their wedding night.

Kody allowed her to walk as far as the door, then swept her off her feet and carried her over the threshold. He kissed her again without putting her down. He crossed to the middle of the great room rising open to the second story.

"Welcome home, Mrs. Douglas," Kody whispered as he set her on her feet. "I have a wedding present for you." He reached into his breast pocket and pulled out a sheaf of official-looking papers, which he unfolded and handed to her.

She read them, tried to make sense of them. "This looks like some kind of business deal."

"Mrs. Murphy offered to sell me the ranch. I can pay it off month by month."

She gaped at him. "She did?"

"Yeah. I guess she likes me."

Chuckling, she kissed him, then tore herself away and turned full circle. "This is to be our home?"

"Think you'll like it?"

She laughed. "It's beautiful. I can hardly wait to see the view through those long windows in daylight."

He pulled her into his arms.

She wrapped her arms around him and hugged him tight. "God is so good."

"That He is." His gentle kiss promised more than enough joy for every day.

Dear Reader,

I like writing about wounded heroes and heroines, but not because I suffered any great hurt in my childhood. I had a lovely, rich childhood and knew God's love from an early age. In adult life, however, I have lived and worked with emotionally damaged people. Not always do they accept the help offered by others and by God. Although I know there are no simplistic answers, I like to imagine how things would be different if injured people could forgive the past and accept God's loving plans for their present and future.

I hope you find encouragement in reading how my characters faced their emotional injuries.

I love to hear from readers. Contact me by e-mail at Linda@lindaford.org. Feel free to check on updates and bits about my research on my Web site: www.lindaford.org.

God Bless,

Linda Ford

QUESTIONS FOR DISCUSSION

1. Where was Kody headed? What did he hope to find there? Was he running to freedom and opportunity or away from something in his past? Did he recognize this?

2. Why was Charlotte alone in the house? Why hadn't she sought help? Are there things in your life that keep you from making a move when you know you need to?

3. What did these two have in common emotionally? Did they understand that? Do you see how others share similar hurts as you? How do you respond to them?

4. Why did Kody think he had to hide his relationship with Star? If you had a chance to talk to him, what suggestions would you like to give him?

5. I see people like Kody and Star on the sidewalks at home—people who feel judged because of who they are or what their choices have been in their lives. I often struggle to feel sympathy for their plight. Do you feel the

same? Does this story help you care a little more about those people we often ignore? If so, what do you think you should do about it? Is God leading you to do something?

6. Kody had loving adoptive parents. Why wasn't it enough for him? What more did he need to be all he could be? Did Charlotte help?

7. Kody faced real prejudice. How did this make Charlotte feel? Who do you identify with most—people like Matron, Charlotte or Kody?

8. There are also people who didn't show prejudice. Why do you think they acted differently even though the feelings of their day supported prejudice? Is there some way God wants you to make a difference today?

9. How did the Dirty 30s affect these characters, or did it? Do we face unique challenges because of the era in which we live? Consider indifference, overload of information, materialism, etc. Are there times we should choose to act contrary to our society's norms?

10. What events caused Kody and Charlotte to

change? Was it a big event or a series of small events? Are you open and paying attention to the small lessons God brings to your life? How do you respond?

11. What further challenges do you think Kody and Charlotte will face? If you could speak to them, what would you want to tell them when they face difficulties?

12. Was there a lesson or encouragement or challenge for you in this story? What was it?

REQUEST YOUR FREE BOOKS!

2 FREE INSPIRATIONAL NOVELS
PLUS 2
FREE
MYSTERY GIFTS

Love Inspired
HISTORICAL
INSPIRATIONAL HISTORICAL ROMANCE

YES! Please send me 2 FREE Love Inspired® Historical novels and my 2 FREE mystery gifts (gifts are worth about $10). After receiving them, if I don't wish to receive any more books, I can return the shipping statement marked "cancel". If I don't cancel, I will receive 4 brand-new novels every other month and be billed just $4.24 per book in the U.S. or $4.74 per book in Canada, plus 25¢ shipping and handling per book and applicable taxes, if any*. That's a savings of over 20% off the cover price! I understand that accepting the 2 free books and gifts places me under no obligation to buy anything. I can always return a shipment and cancel at any time. Even if I never buy another book, the two free books and gifts are mine to keep forever. 102 IDN ERYA 302 IDN ERYM

Name	(PLEASE PRINT)

Address	Apt. #

City	State/Prov.	Zip/Postal Code

Signature (if under 18, a parent or guardian must sign)

Mail to Steeple Hill Reader Service:
IN U.S.A.: P.O. Box 1867, Buffalo, NY 14240-1867
IN CANADA: P.O. Box 609, Fort Erie, Ontario L2A 5X3

Not valid to current subscribers of Love Inspired Historical books.

Want to try two free books from another series?
Call 1-800-873-8635 or visit www.morefreebooks.com

* Terms and prices subject to change without notice. N.Y. residents add applicable sales tax. Canadian residents will be charged applicable provincial taxes and GST. Offer not valid in Quebec. This offer is limited to one order per household. All orders subject to approval. Credit or debit balances in a customer's account(s) may be offset by any other outstanding balance owed by or to the customer. Please allow 4 to 6 weeks for delivery. Offer available while quantities last.

Your Privacy: Steeple Hill Books is committed to protecting your privacy. Our Privacy Policy is available online at www.SteepleHill.com or upon request from the Reader Service. From time to time we make our lists of customers available to reputable third parties who may have a product or service of interest to you. If you would prefer we not share your name and address, please check here. ☐

LIH08R

Love Inspired
HISTORICAL
INSPIRATIONAL HISTORICAL ROMANCE

Adelaide Crum longs for a family, but the closed-minded town elders refuse to entrust even the most desperate orphan to a woman alone. Newspaperman Charles Graves promises to stand by her, despite his embittered heart. Adelaide's gentle soul soon makes him wonder if he can overcome his bitter past, and somehow find the courage to love....

Look for

Courting Miss Adelaide
by
JANET DEAN

*Available September wherever books are sold,
including most bookstores, supermarkets,
drugstores and discount stores.*

Steeple
Hill®

www.SteepleHill.com

LIH82796

Love Inspired.
HISTORICAL

TITLES AVAILABLE NEXT MONTH

Don't miss these two stories in September

FAMILY OF THE HEART by Dorothy Clark
Wealthy heiress Sarah Randolph knows she's not nanny material—but sweet little Nora Bainbridge is in desperate need of mothering. How can she say no? And even though her clashes with haughty widower Clayton Bainbridge urge Sarah to leave, her heart begs her to stay.

COURTING MISS ADELAIDE by Janet Dean
The "orphan train" is Adelaide Crum's last chance for a family. If only the town elders would entrust some children to a single woman! Hope soon appears in the unlikely form of newspaperman Charles Graves. Together, they'll finally learn about family, faith...and love.